I0650322

Henry Harland

Mea Culpa

A woman's last word. Vol. 2

Henry Harland

Mea Culpa
A woman's last word. Vol. 2

ISBN/EAN: 9783337105297

Printed in Europe, USA, Canada, Australia, Japan

Cover: Foto ©Andreas Hilbeck / pixelio.de

More available books at **www.hansebooks.com**

MEA CULPA

A WOMAN'S LAST WORD

BY

HENRY HARLAND

IN THREE VOLUMES

VOL. II.

LONDON

WILLIAM HEINEMANN

1891

[All rights reserved]

I.

ONE morning in June, 1885, my father looked up from a newspaper that he had been reading, and said to me, 'You remember my old friend Léonticheff, Gregory Ivanovitch Léonticheff, do you not, Monica ?'

'Prince Léonticheff? Oh, yes, I remember him,' I answered listlessly.

'You were quite a child when he died. That was in seventy-four. You were about thirteen years old.... And his son, Gabriel, do you remember him ?'

To this I said No; I could not remember Prince Léonticheff's son.

'Gregory Ivanovitch, himself a Prince of

the Empire, and one of the richest noblemen
in Europe, made what his friends considered
rather a misalliance. He married an English-
woman, a sister of Sir Alfonso Luckstone, an
immensely wealthy banker, reputed to be of.
Jewish extraction, but a convert to Christi-
anity. She was a vulgar, loud-voiced creature,
whom, for my part, I could never endure.
Their son, Gabriel Gregoreivitch, was edu-
cated in England, at Eton, and then at
Oxford. It is possible that you never saw
him, though he used to come home for his
holidays. He is a few years your senior,
perhaps now eight or nine and twenty. Yet
already he has contrived to win distinction in
two countries : in England as the author of
several clever novels, and in Russia as one of
the few subjects honoured by the personal
friendship of the Emperor. He is moreover
enormously rich. For, besides the vast
estates that came to him in Russia from his

father, his mother left a very large personal fortune in the English funds. He owns one of the handsomest mansions in London, Salchester House, in Park Lane, described as nothing less than a palace; and he has a fine country-seat, not far from London, on the banks of the Thames, called Argelby Court. . . . I am reminded of all this by a paragraph in *Figaro*, from which I learn that he is in Paris, at the Grand Hôtel. I think I will call upon him. It is of course a slender chance, but if I could interest him in my affair, it would be to gain it. A word from him to the Emperor would be invaluable. He cannot have forgotten the close intimacy that existed between me and his lamented father. Perhaps for the sake of that he will wish to serve me.'

So in the afternoon, having dressed himself with even more scrupulous care than usual, my father went off, to leave his card upon

the young Prince Léonticheff, at the Grand
Hôtel.

While he was away, Armidis came.

The friendship between Armidis and
myself had deepened and ripened a good
deal during the last year and a half, and it
had gained a good deal in seriousness. That
year and a half had been desolate and dreary
enough for me; but it must have been
drearier and more desolate still, except for
Armidis's constant gentle sympathy and
comradeship. Especially during the last five
months! For more than five months I had
not had one line or word from Julian. In
the alternating terror and despair that his
silence caused me, I believe I should have
gone mad, if it had not been for Armidis.
Not that he did anything or said anything to
make the silence less cruel or less ominous;
nobody save Julian himself could have said

or done anything to that effect; but somehow I felt less utterly cast down and forsaken, because of the tender friendship and affection that Armidis in his whole bearing towards me implied, rather than expressed by word of mouth.

Was my lover dead? Or—had he forgotten me?

'Ah, alone? Alone?' cried Armidis, gaily, as he entered the room; and I saw that he was in one of his jaunty, débonnaire moods to-day. 'Where is the Lily? Wherefore has he deserted you?'

I explained the reason of my father's absence.

'Soho! A prince! Gracious goodness me! How swell we are, leaving our cards on Anglo-Russian princes! And Prince Léonticheff at that! Oh, yes, I've read one or two of his novels. Yes, they're unquestionably clever. But prince or peasant, it's the same to me. When I'm in England, I'm a howling snob. In England one can't afford to be anything else. But when I leave England for the Continent, I leave my grovelling worship for rank, wealth, and titles behind me. Prince or peasant, I'm equally thankful for the opportunity I owe him of finding you alone. I'll not disguise it from you, Monica Paulovna, from day to day the society of your venerable parent becomes more and more insupportable to me. If I tolerate him at all, it is simply because he is an inevitable concomitant to you. Every rose has its thorn. From day to day he shrinks visibly further into his armour of selfishness. If it weren't for you, I'd just lavish upon him one solid thundering piece of my mind, and forever after cut him dead. Ouf !'

'Hush !' I protested. ' I cannot allow you to talk like that about my father. You are

utterly unjust, as well as unkind ; and besides, I am his daughter.'

'You're right, quite right. Not in calling
me unjust, but in declaring yourself to be his
daughter. Incredible as it may seem, you
are his daughter; and it's all wrong and
indelicate and in bad taste and everything for
me to abuse him in your presence. But then
I'm not like other girls, you know, and you
must make allowances for the idiosyncrasies
of genius. I take it all back, except the
point. I *am* glad to find you alone.'

He sat down beside me, and took my hand,
and looked into my eyes with a smile so
bright, so sweet, so touching in its determined cheerfulness, that all at once my heart
seemed to melt and go out to him; and then,
involuntarily, before I knew what I was
doing, I began to cry.

He patted my cheek and stroked my hair
with his hand ; and very softly he said,

'That is right, dear. Cry, cry.... It will do you good.'

'Oh, he's dead,' I sobbed wildly. 'I'm sure he's dead. Or else he has forgotten all about me. Oh, I can't bear it, I can't bear it. Oh, what shall I do?'

'There—there—there,' Armidis murmured, as one does to soothe a child. 'No, no, he isn't dead, and he hasn't forgotten you. You pale women with the red hair ... oh, well, not red, if that offends you; we'll call it golden ... you pale women with the eyes and the hair aren't the sort that men forget. You may feel easy in your mind so far as that's concerned. In the whole length and breadth of his horrid old American continent you need fear no rival. I don't mean that you're so handsome, you know; don't delude yourself; but you're so peculiar-looking. Unkind but honest; I was ever thus, a plain blunt man.'

He paused and laughed, and then he went on . . .

'The trouble isn't that he's dead or oblivious; no, no. If you were not the daughter of Paul Mikhaelovitch Banakin,— oh, why do you Russians have such tiresome names?—if you were not the daughter of your father, and if therefore it would not be improper to the last degree for me to do so, I should tell you that I have a private suspicion in the secret places of my own consciousness to the effect that he, the said P. M. B., is at the bottom of the whole mystery. I should say that I powerfully suspect him of having intercepted Mr. North's letters. He found that the affair between you two young people was prolonging itself far, far beyond anything that he had foreseen when he bundled Mr. North off to his native land; and he said to himself that the time had come for him to step in and stop it.

Then, like the practical spirit that he is, he proceeded to put his resolution in operation by pocketing Mr. North's epistles. I should say all this to you, if the gentleman in question were not your father. But by an unfortunate combination of circumstances over which I have no control, he *is* your father. Therefore I say nothing of the kind; but I will call your attention to another theory that perhaps interprets the event equally well.'

He paused again, this time to light a cigarette. After he had sent several voluminous clouds of smoke curling up towards the ceiling, he resumed. . . .

'No, our friend Julian is neither dead nor oblivious, my dear ; but—he is foolish and conscientious. He doesn't get on so rapidly as in the ardour and ignorance of his youth he had hoped to do. He finds that what our French neighbours call the strig-for-lif isn't

the playful little pastime that he had
supposed it would be, but on the contrary
a singularly slow, up-hill, serious piece of
business. He begins to see that instead
of weeks and months, it's likely to be years
and years before he can come back, a capitalist,
to claim your hand... just what your dear
delightful papa saw from the outset, and
which accounted for his sudden and ex-
cessive amiability in getting North shipped
for the wilderness. Finally the foolish and
conscientious young fellow has said to himself, " What right have I, who am I, to
keep that girl with the eyes and the hair
waiting and pining for me all these years, and
wasting her youth over my memory? It
isn't fair. No, no. I must put a period to
it. I mustn't write to her any more, or
remind her of my existence any more. I
must efface myself, and give her a chance to
forget me. Then if I ever do succeed, then

I can go back, and, if the field is still free, try
to win her once again."... That is what he
says to himself, and that's the reason for his
present silence—always assuming that he
really is silent, and that no wicked fairy is
purloining his letters. I understand all this,
because once upon a time I was Anglo-
Saxon myself. By and by he'll realise how
foolish he is. He'll realise that it's perfectly
preposterous to put things off till he's in
receipt of a regular income. Then one
fine day, he'll turn up here in Paris, and
we'll have a Slavo-Yankee wedding, and
we'll all be happy—except possibly Paul
M. Banakin, and he'll have to make the best
of it.'

Oh, no, no, no! I had thought of all this
myself. There was no possible explanation
of Julian's silence that I had not thought
of. In the long miserable days and weeks of
waiting, fearing, hoping, brooding, I had had

ample time to think, and I had thought of
little else. Every imaginable conjecture,
every imaginable suspicion, had passed
through my mind. But by degrees I had
lost my hold upon all of them, save these two:
that he had died, or that he did not love me
any more. I was sure my father had not pur-
loined his letters; he would be incapable of
such cruelty, and doubly incapable of stoop-
ing to a conspiracy with the servants of the
hotel, which would be essential to the success
of any such design. Yet, even that suspicion, unworthy as it was, had occurred to
me . . . No, all that Armidis could say was
powerless to comfort me, or to give me any
new ground for hope; but the deep sweet
kindness that shone from his eyes, and
vibrated in his voice, made my heart grow
big with gratitude and affection.

'Meantime,' he continued, after a little
while, 'we are getting a good deal of ex-

perience. We are learning how true it is
that hope deferred maketh the heart sick, and
we are asking ourselves that old, old question, *Cui bono?* What's the use? It's all
very bitter and discouraging; but it's the
sort of experience that sooner or later, in one
form or another, must come to every man
and woman. If it comes to us a little sooner,
instead of a little later,—why, so we'll get to
the other end of it sooner, and come out
again at the bright side. It's one of the
dismal tunnels through which the way of life is
laid. No one can hope to avoid it... When I
was a young man, in England, years and
years ago, I knew a young girl... But
there! Details are nothing to the point.
I'll not tire you with the story. Some time,
though, when you are at my shop, remind me
of it, and I will show you something.'

'The story won't tire me, I promise you.
Tell it to me,' I pleaded. 'Tell me now.'

'Unless my ears deceive me,' he returned, 'I hear the step of Paul the son of Michael on the stairs. Yes, and his voice. He's not alone. There's some one with him. Who? Not, surely not, his Anglo-Russian Prince. Fancy a prince in the Hôtel du St.-Esprit! But who then? Who else?'

Suddenly, and without any sort of reason, my heart began to palpitate... Could it be...? Oh, no, there was no earthly chance of that : and yet the mere fancy, absurd, impossible, as it was, taking shape in my imagination, made my body tremble, and I could hardly get my breath. I put out my hand, and grasped Armidis's arm.

'Why, mercy upon me, we're all in a tremor!' he exclaimed. 'Oh, you mustn't let yourself hope impossible things, you know.'

'Oh, no, I don't hope anything,' I said. 'I know it's quite impossible. It's only because I am so weak.'

Then my father came into the room. A single glance sufficed to show me that he was in a state of great excitement, of elation. He was accompanied by a young man. ...

'Monica, my daughter,' he began, summoning me. Then, 'Prince, permit me, permit me... I have the honour to present to your Serene Highness my daughter, Monica Paulovna Banakin.'

After which, perceiving Armidis, 'Also, if you will allow me, I beg to present our friend Monsieur Victor Armidis, the composer.'

II.

I MUST endeavour to erase from my mind all that I have since learned of the character of Prince Léonticheff, together with all that long habit has since taught me to see in his appearance, and to set down here as faithfully as possible the first impression that I obtained of him.

I beheld, then, in the person to whom my father, with so much nervous deference, presented me, a tall and rather fat young man, of slouching carriage, and very loosely built, so that his limbs seemed to hang upon him with a certain flabby insecurity, and the effect of his body was gelatinous. He was

dressed with striking and elaborate careless-
ness—in a velvet jacket and waistcoat, and
a dove-coloured flannel shirt, whilst his
necktie was of a flame-red India silk,
fastened in a sailor's knot. His dusty
brown hair, thin on the crown of his head
to the verge of baldness, was cropped as
close as a soldier's or a convict's, so that
everywhere the bluish white of his scalp was
visible. His skin was florid and coarse-
grained, as if it had been exposed a good
deal to the weather. His face was fleshy,
and the lower part of it heavy, merging into
a short fat neck through the medium of an
incipient double chin. His mouth, shaded
by a copious moustache, was unduly long,
the lips being thick and loose; his nose was
short, square, and slightly turned up at the
end. Thus far he was undeniably vulgar-
looking and uncouth; but his forehead was
broad and white and finely modelled, and his

eyes, though set too far in, and not very
big, were blue and pellucid, and full of good-
nature and intelligence. The general effect
of the young man was remote from princely.
'A Russian bear,' I thought to myself. . . .
'An indolent, easy-going, contented fellow,
the son or the grandson of peasants, a little
slow, not a little rough perhaps, but by no
means a fool, and above all things good-
natured,' is probably the guess one would
have made of him. . . . I must not forget
to mention his hands, which, of all his attri-
butes, were perhaps the most unprincely,
being short, blunt-fingered, hirsute, and fiery
red, like the hands of a *commis-voyageur*.

One of these hands he closed upon one of
mine ; and said in a voice that was unreso-
nant and throaty, but soft, caressing, almost
fatherly — speaking slowly, languidly, with
an exceedingly friendly, soothing, ingratiating
inflexion, smiling into my eyes, and keeping

possession of my hand until the end of his speech, — 'I am very glad to meet you again,' he said in English, pronouncing that language not in the least like a foreigner, nor yet like an Englishman, but with an accent quite peculiar to himself, whereby he seemed to fatten and round out the sounds. 'You don't remember me, but I have never forgotten you. I used to catch a glimpse of you now and then when you were a little mite of a girl, and I was a great gawky boy home from school. You were the prettiest little girl I knew, and you made a wonderful impression on me. I think we are going to be friends. We must carry on the tradition of our families. Our fathers were friends, and so were our grandfathers. To tell you the truth, I begin to like you already.'

His bearing, as he said all this, was one of exceeding good nature, of pleasant satis-

faction with himself and everybody else,
and of a comfortable, homely frankness,
which, though comical, was not unprepos-
sessing.

With his last word he gave my hand a
squeeze, released it, and proffered his own
to Armidis, remarking in the same slow,
caressing drawl, 'Well! This is an unex-
pected pleasure. I've heard about you, Mr.
Victor Armidis, and wanted to know you,
any time these ten years. I suppose, between
ourselves, that I'm one of the two or three
most intelligent and most enthusiastic
admirers that you can number. In my
opinion you've done some of the prettiest
little things in the way of lyric music that
this century can show. Why, some of your
songs I wouldn't hesitate to compare to
Schubert's. I'm glad to press your hand.
I believe we are going to like each other.'

'Oh, thank you so much,' returned Armidis

airily. 'You quite cheer me. I'm so pleased to learn that my little things have met with your approval.'

Armidis's querulous irony was plain to see, but the Prince apparently took what he said at the foot of the letter.

'Yes, I'm one of your enthusiastic admirers,' he reiterated. 'And I've given you a puff in *Hilary's Rosary* that will make your fortune for you. You've seen it, of course. No? You haven't? What! Why, it's running as a serial through *Macnaffen's Magazine.* I've quoted a verse from a song of yours, and I've described the melody as one of the nicest and most original little things in modern music. You must get it. It will make you the talk of the day wherever English is read. *Hilary's Rosary!* Why, it's one of the two or three '—he dropped his voice to a key of confidential intimacy, and spoke more slowly than ever, bearing im-

pressively upon each word—' it's one of the
two or three first-rate novels that have been
done in the English language. It deals
with Irish patriotism ; and apart from its interest as fiction, it contains more authentic
information about Ireland than any other
dozen books put together. And then, the
plot! You never saw anything prettier.
And the characters...! And the workman-
ship, the style...! Why, my friend'—he
patted Armidis gently upon the shoulder, to
lend emphasis to his words—' my friend,
when the serial publication of *Hilary's
Rosary* is finished, and the book comes out
in three volumes, the people, the People, are
going to rise up and greet it as the best thing
since Harry Fielding.'

He made this surprising statement with
perfect gravity, and not a touch of embar-
rassment or misplaced humility. He recom-
mended his own novel with the same serene,

impersonal earnestness, the same quiet, confidential assurance, that he might have
employed in advising us to read one of the
acknowledged masterpieces of Tolstoi or
Turghéneff.

This struck me as strange at the time;
his speech lacked verisimilitude, and I almost
mistrusted my ears; but before long I came
to understand it. Prince Léonticheff was a
clever, in some respects even an able man;
upon certain subjects — for example, Irish
history and Anglo-Irish politics — he was
really profoundly well-informed; he could
write novels that enjoyed a great vogue in
England, were pirated in America, and
translated into three or four foreign tongues;
he was a high contracting party in the world
of finance, being the power behind the sign
in the great international banking-house of
Luckstone Brothers; and with all the rest
he had somehow known how to acquire

the personal friendship and confidence of the
most suspicious monarch in Europe ; surely
he must have been a man of remarkable
abilities.   Yet, as I soon came to realise, he
had not one scintilla of the sense of humour!
Not the first meagre rudiment of it.   In consequence, he was enabled to give himself up
with unreserve to that tendency innate in
every individual consciousness (which a sense
of humour—that is to say, a sense of proportion and of congruity—can alone correct),
to regard itself as the centre of the Universe,
and as the biggest, the most vital, the most
important Fact.   The results of this absence
of humour upon Prince Léonticheff's speech
and conduct were often queer ; sometimes
they were appalling.

'Now,' he went on, turning to me, 'I
have come over here with your good father,
to take you off to dinner with me.   First we
go for a drive, a little spin about the Bois,

and that sort of thing, to whet our appetites ;
then we dine at the Ambassadeurs, where I
have engaged a private room with a balcony.
Your father tells me that you've lived five or
six years here in Paris, without once dining
at the Ambassadeurs. He thought it
wouldn't be proper. Why, bless your soul,
you just lower your veil as you pass in and
out ; and who's the wiser ? I've—this is
between ourselves—I've dined some of the
first ladies of Europe at the Ambassadeurs :
yes, the Princess ——, and the Countess
of * * *, and Lady † † † ; and they've come
away delighted. Now go put on your hat.
My trap is waiting at the door... Of
course, you are with us,' he added, nodding
to Armidis. ' I want to hear you talk.
People have described you to me as one of
the wittiest men of your generation. I want
to see for myself whether you deserve your
reputation.'

'Oh, really? Do people speak so kindly of me? Oh, how nice!' murmured Armidis, with a smile that was not devoid of malice. 'Oh, yes, thank you, I'm with you. People have never described you to me at all, but already I begin to perceive that you are immensely unusual and curious. I shall be quite charmed.'

The trap that we found waiting at the door, in charge of two gigantic powdered footmen, gorgeously liveried in buff and gold and scarlet, was an odd affair. The Prince directed our attention to its peculiarities, explaining, 'It's a little thing of my own invention. One of the most remarkable facts about me is that I have a strongly developed genius for mechanics. I made the model for it with my own ten fingers, and then had it built under my supervision.'

Its peculiarity consisted in its having only

one seat, which, however, was ample to accommodate five people, being curved like a horse-shoe.

' It is the application of the amphitheatrical idea to a carriage,' said the inventor. ' It's like the stern-sheets of a boat. You see, I sit here in the middle, where the skipper of the boat would sit, only, instead of a tiller, I hold the reins. Then my guests distribute themselves to my right and left. The advantage is that we all face one another, and can talk together, and yet no one has to sit with his back to the horses.'

The body of the vehicle was painted black, with an immense, flamboyant coat-of-arms and coronet emblazoned on it; the wheels were crimson. It was drawn by three superb white horses, one leader, and two wheelers abreast; and there was a foot-board behind for the flunkies. A decidedly conspicuous equipage; and numberless were

the people who turned to stare at us, as
we went dashing through the Boulevard St.-
Germain, across the Pont and Place de la
Concorde, and up the Avenue des Champs
Elysées.

Though his horses were spirited, and
demanded a good deal of management, the
Prince, who seemed to be a skilful driver,
talked incessantly.   He talked exclusively
about himself, and always in his slow, simple,
good-natured way.

'I came here to Paris incog.,' he informed
us.   'I've got a nice little house of my own
in the Avenue Malakoff, as I suppose you
know; but I went to the Grand Hôtel, and
gave my name as George Lyons.   It was no
go, though.   Somebody there recognised
me, and betrayed me to the newspapers.   I
was a good deal annoyed at that, because the
business that brings me here is of a very
secret nature, and I can't afford to let it be

known that I'm in it. Just between
ourselves, I'll say that there's an important
newspaper for sale, and that I'm thinking of
buying it. Not in my own name, no, no.
But I wanted to look into its affairs, and if I
concluded it was worth while, I'd buy it
through a dummy. To say nothing of its
usefulness, I know few things more amusing
than to control a newspaper. I suppose you
know who owns the *London Beacon?*
Prince Gigi, my friends.'

'Gigi...?' repeated my father, interro-
gatively.

'Yes. Didn't you know? That's my
nick - name : Gigi, — G. G., — Gabriel
Gregoreivitch. Good, isn't it?... But as
I was saying, when you interrupted me,
there's a law of compensations; and when I
knew the murder was out, I made up my
mind to stay, and to go in for some fun.
Oh, I know how to amuse myself in Paris... `

Besides, if it hadn't been for those annoying little paragraphs in the newspapers, I shouldn't have had the pleasure of meeting you. You only got hold of it in this morning's *Figaro;* but the first of the series appeared in the *Petit Journal* more than a week ago ... I passed the winter at St. Petersburg, which was very cold and gay. Then at Easter I went on to London, where I've been stopping ever since. I suppose you know, I own the nicest house in London, Salchester House, in Park Lane. I bought it about five years ago, after the death of the last of the Lords Salchester. It's big, and yet it's pretty and comfortable, and I like it. But there's nothing under the sun that bores me like a London Season ; the people are so methodical, and business-like, and con-scientious in their dissipations. And yet in one way it amuses me a good deal. I do enjoy seeing your steady-going English

prigs, who in their secret hearts regard me
very much as if I were the devil himself, I
do enjoy seeing them swallow their prudery
and pocket their scruples, and pay homage
to my rank and wealth. Of course there's
the fast set ; but that's different ; they
imitate me ; but I'm speaking of your steady-
going, highly moral people, like the ***s,
and the †††s. They've never got over the
shock my famous little escapade at Oxford
caused them ; and they don't like my attitude
towards the Irish Question ; and they think,
because I'm bluff and hearty and condescend-
ing in my manners, that I'm vulgar and
lacking in dignity ; and my reputation as a
gambler sends cold shivers down their
spines. Yet I'm a Serene Highness, you
know, and a Prince of the Russian Empire,
and so they throw their houses open to me,
and their daughters at my head. It's
interesting. The only people I really like in

London are those whom I call *la haute
Bohême:* theatrical people, Irish Members,
journalists, and that sort.   And the only club
I care for is the X... I like that club
because the men you meet there are men,
masculine, virile, not effete, like the
members of the Y... and Z..., and not
afraid of a good story, or a song, or a bottle
of wine.   Speaking of my attitude towards
the Irish Question, that's a funny thing
about me, and a good many people can't
understand it : how, whereas in Russia I'm
the most intense sort of a Reactionary, in
England I do all I can in a quiet way to
help on the cause of Irish Home Rule.
Well, it's the simplest and the most natural
thing in the world.   The Irish people and
the Russian people are as different as dogs
and horses ; and what's meat for one would
be poison for the other.   But it puzzles the
general public, and makes talk, and affords

me a great deal of amusement. I suppose
you follow my leaders in the *Beacon*. No?
Oh, you must, you must. One appears
every Wednesday and every Saturday, when
Parliament is sitting, and they're by all
means the strongest things on the Irish
Question that are printed nowadays,—
though, of course, it isn't officially known that
I write them; that wouldn't do; might lead
to international complications. I suppose
I know more about the history of Ireland and the actual needs and conditions
of the Irish, than any other living man...
Well, that brings me back to what I was
saying of my reputation as a gambler. The
truth of the matter is simply this. I'm a
thoroughbred Russian; and so there's
nothing that fascinates me like a game of
chance: roulette, dice, black-and-red: it
doesn't matter which. And I'm rich enough
to afford to lose, and therefore I play. And

I'd just be glad to hear anybody prove that it's immoral. I'm rich enough to lose without grumbling, and I do lose almost invariably. Why, I suppose my average annual losses would foot up something like four or five thousand pounds. And I know of no other way in which the same amount of money could buy me the same amount of pleasure. Therefore I want to know why I shouldn't play? Are you acquainted with the beautiful little American institution called draw-poker? Well, at poker alone, last month, I lost between six and seven hundred. With that bad luck at cards, you say, unless there's no truth in the proverb, I ought to be an extraordinarily fortunate young man in love. Well, perhaps I am. Ho-ho-ho!'

And the Prince suspended his discourse, to indulge in a long, loud, boisterous laugh.

At the Café des Ambassadeurs he said, ' One of the funny things about me is my

capacity for champagne. It's practically
boundless. I can drink enough champagne
at one sitting to put any other three men
under the table, and never know it then
or the next day. But the remarkable part
of it is this: if I touch any other wine,
or any spirits, I'm done for quicker than
powder and shot.'

He also appeared to have a considerable
capacity for food; and between the courses
of the dinner he smoked numberless fat
cigarettes.

When the coffee was served, he looked
at his watch.

'Hello!' he cried. 'Half-past ten. And
I've got an engagement for eleven which I
can't possibly neglect. I'll have barely time
now to run into my hotel, put on my dress-
suit, and keep it. So I'm afraid we'll have
to break up. But we must meet again to-
morrow. There are lots of things I want

to say to you, and lots of questions I want to
ask you. Besides, I want to get thoroughly
well acquainted with you. I like you—all of
you. But you,'—nodding to Armidis,—
'you've disappointed me. You've scarcely
opened your mouth once since I met you,
and the reason I invited you to join us
was that I wanted to hear you talk. Perhaps
we'll get on better to-morrow. You,'—
addressing my father, — 'you come and
breakfast with me to-morrow at noon. We
will talk things over, and make some arrange-
ment for the evening. I think I'd like to
dine at some little Bohemian restaurant in
your Latin Quarter; and afterwards perhaps
we'll go to the play... Good-night, good-
night.'

'Well, is he not refreshing?' demanded my
father, when we had parted from him. 'So
simple, so natural, so unspoilt, so—there is

but one word for it—so primitive. So
unlike your conventional child of the century.
What frankness, what *bonhomie !* I feel ten
years younger for the hours I have passed
in his company. And so friendly ! He has
promised to read the manuscript of my History of Russia, and I count upon him to find
me a publisher. I have not yet spoken to
him of my appeal to the Emperor ; but I am
sure he will interest himself in it. Oh, he is
the most refreshing personality I have encountered for many a long year.'

'He is a very surprising character, with
his barbarism, his clumsiness, his incredible
vanity, his boundless admiration for himself.
His bragging was funny at first, but it grew
rather tiresome towards the end. I think I
never saw anybody so absolutely deficient
in tact. But he's apparently harmless and
good-natured enough,' said I.

'Oh, dear, oh, dear !' complained Armidis.

'How can people show so little penetration?
He's a great big lump of cheap vulgarity
and piggish selfishness. A prince, forsooth!
A lout, a boor, a bully, a cad! Simple,
natural, primitive? So is a wild boar. Good-
natured? Oh, wow-wow! Say satisfied,
complacent, if you please. So is any other
animal, when its appetites are gratified and
the weather's fine. But don't say *good-*
natured. Why, consider his jaw and chin.
He's a great big monster of dogged, sordid,
sodden egotism, as brutal as a rhinoceros, as
cruel and remorseless as all beasts are in a
state of nature. Why, the Pachyderm! He's
not really conscious that anything or any
person exists outside of his own thick hide.
Egotism! The concentrated essence of
egotism. A monumental bulk of egotism,
slow-moving, ponderous, certain to crush
every lighter body that may come between it
and its objective point. Ugh! I never saw

a more repulsive brute.   How can—how *can*
you tolerate him ?   The Turk !'

'Mercy on me, what a tirade,' said my
father.   ' You are angry with him because he
snubbed you.'

And I must confess that I myself thought
Armidis uncharitable and unjust.

III.

'HERE,' said Prince Léonticheff, addressing
me, when, escorted by my father, he entered
our room the next afternoon; and he offered
me a brown paper parcel, in size and shape
resembling an octavo book. 'This good
friend'—laying his hand upon my father's
shoulder—'tells me that you translate novels
into French. Well, then, I'm just the man
you want to talk with. I've got a novel
here that's going to make a sensation throughout the civilized world. This is my manuscript in English. It's a thing I've been
at work on for upwards of ten years; ever
since I was a boy; not steadily, of course,

but from time to time, as the inspiration seized me. I finished it about a month ago. It's short, simple, unpretentious, and I suppose the most poetical thing in English prose. Yes, or German, either, for the matter of that. When I tell you that it's better than *Undine*, you'll get some idea of how tremendously good it is. The central thought, the theme, is one that Goethe would have given all he ever wrote to have got hold of.... Open the parcel, and look at the title-page.'

He took the parcel from my hand, and opened it.

' You've never seen my manuscript before,' he said. ' Isn't it pretty? I suppose I write at once the daintiest and the most characteristic hand of any living author.'

The manuscript was indeed pretty, and his hand was indeed dainty and full of individuality, being almost microscopically small, yet as clear and as regular as print.

'A good many people think it's like Thackeray's,' he went on. 'But if you'll take the trouble to compare the two, you'll see that mine is more legible and more elegant. I write very rapidly, yet there's never a blot, an erasure, or an illegibility, on a single page. Isn't my title stunning? Read it out. Read it aloud. I want to hear you read it aloud.'

I obediently read from his title-page: ' Drachensnest : the Bishop and the Witch : being the True History of Zillah, Wife of Barzillai-Ben-Ascher, called the Witch of Drachensnest, and of Alvin, Bishop of Drachensnest : now first set forth in English by Prince Léonticheff.'

'Splendid, splendid !' he cried, clapping his hands. 'Why, that title is a little master-piece. And you read it beautifully, per-

fectly.... Well, now, I'm going to leave
this manuscript with you. Take good care
of it, for it's worth considerably more than
its weight in gold. I'm going to leave it
with you, and I want you to study it. You
couldn't get the full flavour of it by a single
reading. You must read it straight through
at least three times. Then you'll know it,
you'll feel it, you'll catch the enthusiasm of
it. After that, when you're thoroughly im-
bued with it, I want you to translate it. I
want you to translate it from my manuscript
under my supervision. Then I'll publish
it simultaneously in French and English ;
and instead of your getting a beggarly little
four hundred francs for a translation, you'll
get half of what I receive for the original
French work. I shall take it to Calmann
Lévy, and sell it to him as an original work,
which it will be in point of fact, not having
previously appeared in any other language,

and I'll give you half of all that he pays me.
I translated my last novel myself, and it
was published simultaneously here and in
London; and you'd be amazed if I should
tell you what Lévy gave me for the French
rights.... Now you take it, and study it,
and let me know whether you think you'll be
able to do it justice. Of course you must
translate it *con amore*, or it won't do. I
could put in the fine touches for you, and
that sort of thing, but I'd need a good basis
of nice literature to work on. The ordinary
hack translation would answer well enough
for an ordinary novel, but not for a little
chef-d'œuvre like this.'

I replied that I should be very glad to
read it, but that I feared I should not be
able to make the sort of translation that he
desired, for I could write none but an un-
polished and unliterary French, a French
that would pass muster well enough in an

ordinary hack translation, but would never answer the demands for style which the French public would make upon an original work. I said this first because it was the truth ; and secondly because I suspected that Prince Léonticheff, with his high opinion of his own production, would be a difficult man for even a master of French style to satisfy . . . .

I was, accordingly, a good deal relieved, when he returned, 'Well, in that case, of course, you'd better not attempt it. I'm sorry, because I was glad of the chance to give you an opportunity to make some money. However, I'll leave the manuscript with you, anyhow ; only do take great care of it. You'll enjoy reading it, as you probably haven't enjoyed a work of fiction for a long while. I can see that you've got taste, and can tell a good thing when you find it. Oh, it's a little jewel, a little pearl !

I'll try to arrange to come here say to-morrow afternoon, and then you can read it aloud to me.'

I dare say it looks like exaggeration, but I pledge my word that it is literally true. If I have not exactly repeated his speech, letter for letter, I have mitigated rather than accentuated it. And I am sure that I have faithfully rendered the spirit of it: that third-personal, objective delight in his own creation, and admiration of it, which his singular temperament enabled him to enjoy.

'But I say,' he demanded, sweeping our room and our faces with an inquiring glance, 'where's your eccentric friend Armidis? I expected to find him here. Isn't he the most ridiculous looking creature that was ever allowed at large? A peripatetic rag-bag! I should like to give him a decent suit of clothes. But I don't suppose it's want of money that causes him to make such a guy of himself; it's more probably vanity, a desire to be peculiar, conspicuous, to attract attention. Pity he's got that small weakness, because he really is a man of capital talent. I want to see more of him. I've been told that he's a great character, very amusing, a good talker, but a little cracked in the upper storey. I may find him useful some time, when I need an eccentric personage for a novel. Aren't you expecting him to turn up here for dinner? I thought I made it clear last night that I wanted you all to dine with me again to-day.'

'I don't know,' said my father. 'He may come. But he is not a person whom one can feel at all sure of. He always does the thing you least expect. He may come, he may not. It's an even chance.'

The Prince's face flushed red, and his voice grew loud and harsh. . . . 'But didn't he understand that I wanted him? Didn't I make that plain enough? I don't like to be treated in this cavalier manner.'

'Oh, I am sure he could never intend to treat your Serene Highness cavalierly,' put in my father, hastening to appease the Prince's wrath. 'It is most likely that he did not understand himself to be included in your invitation.'

'Well, then, he must be pretty obtuse,' said the Prince.

'He is not obtuse,' said I, rather bluntly. 'He is the least obtuse of men. But he is extremely independent and unusual. You must take him as he is, or not at all.'

'Well, anyhow, I want him,' said the Prince; 'and I'll tell you what. Where does he live? I'll go and fetch him. There's plenty of time. It isn't six o'clock yet, and we shan't want to dine before eight. Give me his address.'

My father mentioned Armidis's address.

but added, 'I'm afraid it is a very slim chance that you will find him at home.'

'Never mind,' the Prince rejoined, now again all good-nature. 'I'll try the experiment. You stay here, and if he comes while I'm gone, keep him. You'—nodding to me—'you come with me. Your father won't object; will you, Banakin? I want to have a talk with you. Nobody will know who you are. And the drive will do you good. Go, put on your bonnet.'

Prince Léonticheff, at that moment, struck me as the most tiresome person I had ever known, and I shrank from the notion of a drive with him. I looked for rescue to my father. That he, a most punctilious stickler for the proprieties, would sanction the Prince's proposition, I never so much as dreamed. For me, an unmarried woman, to go about the streets of Paris alone in a carriage with a young man!

But to my surprise, and equally to my regret, my father demanded sharply, 'Well? Well? Have you not heard? Go put on your bonnet.'

There was no help for it. Prince Léonticheff was a man whom, for my father's sake, I must not offend. And now that my father had said yes, I could not very graciously say no.

A simple Victoria, drawn by a single horse, and driven by a coachman in plain black livery, stood in front of the Hôtel du St.-Esprit.

'It is sometimes a relief,' said the Prince, when he had helped me into this vehicle, 'to put aside the pomp and splendour by which I am usually surrounded, and to go in for a little quiet, unostentatious comfort. On the whole, I thoroughly enjoy being a prince and a millionaire. I enjoy the romance of it,

the celebrity, the luxury, and the power.
Some very rich or very illustrious men are
always tormented by the suspicion that
nobody really likes them for themselves, and
that the people who are pleasant and cordial
to them are all toadies, and have ulterior
designs—axes to grind, as the saying is.
But I consider that morbid and unreasonable. No such fancy ever disturbs me. I
know I'm a nice, good-natured fellow, a good
talker, a hearty companion, and I don't see
why people *shouldn't* like me for myself, just
as well as they would if I were a pauper or a
nonentity. Of course there are a certain
number of people whom I can single out
instantly as mere favour-hunters and syco-
phants : I have very delicate instincts and
intuitions ; but when all is said, they're an
insignificant minority. The great mass of
the people who make themselves agreeable
to me, do so because they like me. I know

that to be a fact, because I've gone around
a good deal incog., and I've been just as well
treated then, as when I've sailed under my
true colours. Understand ?'

'Yes,' I said, 'I understand.'

'Well, that's the long and the short of the
matter: I enjoy my wealth and my rank
immensely, but only on the condition that I
can step down and become a common every-
day man among men whenever the whim
seizes me. Now to-day, you see, I've quite
put aside all pomp and circumstance, and am
driving about in a one-horse Victoria, like
any bourgeois. I suppose the people that
see us pass, think I'm some prosperous
shop-keeper, or a notary, or something,
eh ?'

'Yes, very likely,' I said, feeling that he
expected me to say something.

'You know,' he went on, 'it's generally
believed that a really extraordinary man is

always extraordinary in more ways than one.
Well, look at me. I'm extraordinary first as
one of the two or three richest and most
eminent noblemen in Europe; then, if you
please, as one of the shrewdest and most
influential financiers; then as one of the most
extravagant and reckless *viveurs;* finally as
perhaps the ablest living novelist, and
certainly the ablest writing in English. The
consequence is that wherever I go, I'm
pointed out: here as his Serene Highness
Prince Léonticheff; there as the chief of
the great house of Luckstone Brothers;
elsewhere as the author of *The Weird
Sovereign;* elsewhere still as Prince Gigi,
the dare-devil man of the world. It's great
fun, and I don't know why I should pretend
not to enjoy it. If there's anything that I
hate and abominate, it is false modesty and
affectation.'

'They are indeed abominable qualities,' I

admitted. 'I don't think you can ever be
accused of them.'

'I should hope not. . . . But now don't
let's talk any more about me ; I want to talk
to you about yourself and your father. The
poor old man has been telling me to-day the
whole story of his misfortunes : of how you
had to take French leave of your home in
St. Petersburg, of the sort of life that you've
been living here in Paris, and of the efforts
that he's been making to bring his case and
his wrongs to the notice of the Emperor.
He's a great talker, as you know; and I've
let him talk away to his heart's content all
the afternoon. Among other things he told
me of the unfortunate attachment you had
formed for that young American painter . . .
what's his name. . . .'

'*Prince Léonticheff !*' I cried. My heart
was pounding, and my cheeks felt on fire.
'Oh, how could my father have been so. . . . !'

'So what? Why, your father was all
right. He told it to me in the natural course
of conversation, and I was very glad he did
so, because. . . .'

'I must beg you,' I interrupted, trying to
control my pain and my excitement, and to
speak calmly and with dignity, 'whatever my
father may have said to you, I must beg you,
in the name of decency and delicacy, not to
speak of it to me. I cannot listen to another
word.'

'Oh, come, now! Don't be angry. You
must understand that I'm a good many years
older than you, and besides, that I'm probably
the best friend you and your father have got
in the world. I think you're a little heroine,
and I like you and respect you. What's
more, I'm going to help you. The sort of
life that you're leading here is all wrong, and
wicked, and wasteful. You weren't born to
spend your days giving music lessons, or

translating fifth-rate novels. You'll never be young but once, and youth is too precious a thing to be allowed to slip away unused. I'm your true friend and your father's; and I'm going to help you. But first you must let me speak my mind freely and frankly, or else we can't reach any common ground of understanding. Now, then, to return to what I was going to say about your attachment for the young American painter....'

My feelings of resentment, of outrage, of confusion, were so intense, I could hardly command my voice. It cost me a great effort to say, ' I have asked you, Prince Léonticheff, not to speak to me of that. I do not know how I can prevent you, if you choose to take advantage of my helplessness to defy my wishes. I can't jump out of your carriage; I can't make myself deaf. But it does not seem to me exactly—I will not say gentle-manlike—but manly, on your part. I thought

no one but a coward would take advantage
of a woman's helplessness.'

'Why, but look here. I'm not taking any
advantage of you. What I want to say
won't hurt you. On the contrary, it's something that will be entirely to your benefit to
hear. It's of the highest possible importance
that I should say it to you, for your father's
sake. He asked me to say it to you. I said
it to him, and he said he wished I would say
the same thing to you. You. . . .'

'Anything I need to hear for my father's
sake, I prefer to hear from my father's lips.
I must remind you that you are a stranger to
me. I cannot allow you to speak to me
about my private affairs.'

'Oh, I say, Miss Banakin! You mustn't
think of me as a stranger. I've known you
ever since your childhood, and I'm your
devoted friend. I am more anxious than I
can tell you to be of use to you, to help your

father to be reinstated in his rights as a
Russian noble. But to that end there are
certain things which it is absolutely necessary
should be said. And I think it's weak and
unworthy and unwomanly on your part to
refuse to hear them, because they happen to
be a little disagreeable. You tell me you'd
rather hear them from your father. That's
all very well, but, as he and I agreed this
afternoon, you wouldn't believe them if your
father said them to you. You'd doubt
whether he knew what he was talking about ;
you'd think he was influenced in his opinions
by his personal feelings. But you know that
I have no personal feelings in the matter,
and furthermore, that I can speak with
authority, as one who knows. What I want
to say won't hurt you. It's my duty as your
friend to say it. Can't you sink your own
little individual feelings for a moment, and
look upon me as a sort of elder brother, and

let me advise you ? The amount of it is, I
can't be of any earthly assistance to your
father, if I'm not to be allowed to say my say
to you.'

I bit my lips, and kept silence.

'You don't imagine, I hope,' he went on,
'that I am actuated by any other motive than
a desire to serve you ? It's delicate ground ;
and if it is painful for you to hear me, can't
you understand that it isn't altogether delightful for me to have to say it ?... Come,
I want you to tell me what selfish motive I
could possibly have.'

'Oh, I suppose your motives are well
enough,' I answered sullenly. 'But there
are some things that no motives can
justify.'

'Quite so. There are. And now do you
want me to tell you one thing that no motive
can justify ? It's for a young girl, just for
the sake of her small personal pleasure,

to refuse to listen to a man who has matters
of the highest importance to discuss with
her.'

I made no further resistance. Detestable
as it would be for me to hear him, perhaps I
had better do so. It was true, in a way,
that I had no right to let my personal
pleasure or displeasure stand between Prince
Léonticheff and his willingness or his ability
to serve my father. I was hot with hurt
and shame and anger; but I sat motionless
and speechless, keeping my eyes turned
away from him, and tried to console myself
by thinking that words break no bones.

'Now, then,' he said, 'I will be short and
direct. I say of your attachment for the
young American—I can't recall his name;
something like West—I say it's an unfortunate attachment; and so it is, for more
reasons than one. It's unfortunate, first and
foremost, because it can't possibly come to

anything, the young man being penniless, and you being in a position where you can't afford to marry a poor man. It's furthermore unfortunate because, unless all signs fail, the young man has been inconstant; anyhow, he has stopped writing to you, and is allowing you to break your heart for him in solitude. But finally and chiefly, and if for no other reason, it's unfortunate, because the most effective step that you could take to damn eternally your father's cause in Russia would be to form an alliance with an American.'

He paused for a moment, as if to give this announcement time to sink into my brain. Then he continued. . . .

'You see, it's this way. Of course, what you and your father want to do more than anything else just now is to give the impression at Court, that in spite of the harsh and unjust treatment that you've received,

you remain true and loyal subjects. Therefore you couldn't marry a foreigner without
asking the Emperor's permission ; and I can
assure you of this — the Emperor would
never sanction a marriage between your
father's daughter and a citizen of the United
States. If your father had kept his mouth
shut, and refrained from committing his
thoughts on the subject of republicanism to
paper, it would be an entirely different
matter. But among the manuscripts that
were found in his possession when your
house was searched, was a lucubration in
which he declared a republic to be the only
rational form of human government ; and it
was that which did as much as anything
else to determine his condemnation to Siberia
as an untrustworthy person. Well, now, if he
applied for leave to marry his daughter to
an American citizen, a republican *par excel-
lence*, you may imagine the impression that

would be made in Russia. No, no; you
must give up thinking of your young
American, you must cure yourself of your
interest in him. You can do it, if you'll
try. I know by experience that it's a possible, almost an easy thing, to cure one's
self of an affection that is inimical to one's
welfare; and you must do it.... *V'là,*
that's all I had to say on the subject of
your love-affair. You see it wasn't anything very terrible, and you've survived
it.'

He seemed to expect me to say something by way of rejoinder or acknowledg-
ment, but as I held my tongue, he presently
resumed. . . .

'For the rest, I may tell you in three
words that I am going to cause you and
Paul Mikhaelovitch to be reinstated in all
your rights and privileges at home. It's
going to be a difficult and no doubt a lengthy

undertaking. But I was never known to fail in anything I seriously attempted, and I don't mean to fail in this. If we don't succeed at once, we'll succeed later; and if one method fails us, we'll try another. But we'll win in the end. You were never born to be a poor miserable music-teacher on the wrong side of the Seine; you're too high-born and too high-bred, you're too pretty and too nice. You were born to shine in the great world, and to adorn a noble home. You see I'm blunt and bluff, and I don't mince matters or construct fine phrases. I speak out my mind in the first and the simplest words that come to me. But I want you to believe, Miss Banakin, that my heart is in the right place, and that I've conceived a deep and genuine fondness for you and your father, and that you may count upon me as your firm and devoted friend. I want to hear you say that you believe me.'

'Oh, yes, I believe you,' I said awkwardly, and not too cordially.

'Good. Well, then, as I've told you, I'm going to put an end to the sort of life that circumstances are compelling you to lead at present. But first — and this is another point of supreme importance—first I've got to persuade you to join me in influencing your poor dear father to sacrifice something that's as precious to him as your young American painter was to you. You know what I mean?'

'No, I do not,' I said.

'Why, this so-called History of Russia that he's been wasting his time over for I don't know how many years. In the first place, there's only one man living who knows enough of it to write a History of Russia, and that man's not your father. But, in the second place, this thing that he has written would give mortal offence in the very quarter where he most needs to curry favour—I mean in the Imperial palace. Of course it's not likely that he could ever find a publisher insane enough to undertake the expense of printing it ; but if he should, his last chance of pardon from the throne would be knocked from under him. He's been reading me scraps of it this afternoon, and explaining his point of view, and developing his little theories. I told him plainly that I thought he was mad.... Well, what I want you to do is to join me in urging him to burn it. When you've given up your young American painter, and your father has burned his so-called History of Russia, the rest will be, comparatively speaking, plain sailing.'

My American painter ! There was little need for me to give him up. It was he who had already given me up. Yet one by one

the words that Prince Léonticheff spoke
seemed to sink into my heart like drops of
molten iron, burning out the last shred of
hope that was left there, filling it with a
deathly pain and despair.

Oh, Julian! Oh, God help me!

We found Armidis, and brought him away.
Then we stopped at the Hôtel du St.-Esprit
for my father, and went to dine at the
Restaurant Foyot. Somehow it seemed to
me that I had never in all my life before
been so unhappy as I was to-night. I could
not have told why, perhaps, but it was so.
Something cold and heavy, like a ball of
ice, weighed in my breast and made it ache.
It was as if I had received through some
sixth sense a vague, occult warning of danger
at hand, of approaching sorrow greater than
any that I had known as yet. Armidis talked
a vast deal to-night, but I could not interest

myself in what he said, nor smile at his pleasantries. I remember, though, this little passage at arms between him and Prince Léonticheff...

The Prince cried out, 'By Jove, you are the most amusing character I've ever met. I'm going to write a novel, just for the sake of putting you in.'

'Your Serene Highness had better not attempt it,' Armidis retorted. 'It's been tried a great many times, but it can't be done. I am the rock upon which so many of my novel-writing friends have made shipwreck. I'm quite *insaisissable.*'

'Don't be too sure of that, my friend,' said the Prince. 'One of the remarkable facts about me—and you mustn't allow yourself to forget it—is that what I succeed in, most men have tried and failed in.'

I believed Prince Léonticheff to be, for all his vulgarity, his self-conceit, his ponderosity, his lack of tact and humour, an honest, kind-hearted, well-meaning man, and a true friend and valuable ally of my father's. But to-night the sight of his fat face and burly figure, the sound of his unctuous, husky voice, were infinitely distasteful, even hateful to me. I dare say it was not his fault, however. The light and the savour had gone out of the world. Everything was bitter or insipid to my palate. In my dull, sick languor the only thing I wished for— but for that I wished intensely—was to get away, home, in my own room, alone, alone with my dreary thoughts, my dead hopes, my bruised, bleeding love. It was, I suppose, the instinct of the sick animal to slink off and suffer its dull misery in hiding.

At last we rose from table. Armidis and the Prince walked with us to the door of our hotel. There they bade us good-night, and went away together.

'*Eh bien*, my daughter, I consider my cause gained,' said my father. 'For only a little while longer shall we be forced to lead this wretched Bohemian existence. The Prince has come to our rescue, like the gallant nobleman he is. In a few weeks this shabby lodging-house will see the last of us. We shall be speeding towards St. Petersburg, in a *train de luxe*, there to resume our proper station in the world.'

At these words, somehow, the grief that was pent up in me seemed to find an outlet. I burst into tears.

'Oh, father, father,' I sobbed, 'why should we make a change? Are we not well enough here? We have lived here so long, we are so accustomed to our way of living. We have plenty; we are not uncomfortable. The thought of breaking up, and going away, and making a change for the unknown—oh, it terrifies me. Let us be contented, and go on living our quiet, simple life. Oh, I wish Prince Léonticheff had never come to us. I wish we had never seen him. Let him go away, and leave us as he found us.'

My father stood as still as a statue, and looked at me with amazement, with stupefaction, in his eyes.

At last he gave his head a toss, and cried, 'What is this I hear? Is it that you do not know what you are saying? Is it that you are mad?'

'Oh, no, I am not mad. I know what I say, and I mean it. I can't bear the thought of this complete breaking up and changing of our life. It frightens me. I don't like Prince Léonticheff. I don't like to think of him entering into our private affairs, and determining them for us. It all makes me feel uneasy and full of terror. He may be a very good man in his way, but he is not of our kind. Oh, don't let us put ourselves under such an obliga-

tion to him. Oh, if he would only go away,
if we only might never see him any more !'

'Well, if you are not mad,' said my father,
'then you are selfish to a degree that seems
incredible. You, who are young and strong,
you have adapted yourself to this that you
call our quiet simple life; but which I call
our mean, shabby, precarious life : a hand-to-
mouth existence humbler than that of the
smallest bourgeois. You have adapted yourself to it, you have even come, it appears, to
like it, to enjoy it. But I . . . ? Can you not
consider me a little? Just Heaven! Has
my daughter sunken so low ? And does she
desire to bind me, to chain me, to her own
low level ?'

He ceased speaking for a few seconds, and
marched backwards and forwards once or
twice through the room. I sat still in my
place, weeping silently. All at once he
began again . . .

' I must do you the justice of assuming that
you have not thought, that you have not
considered, that you have spoken upon the
blind impulse of the moment. You are young
and strong. But I ... ? I am old, I am far
from well. I grow appreciably older, I grow
appreciably feebler, from day to day. My
powers of resistance become daily less. From
my cradle until I am fifty, I am habituated to
every luxury that our Nineteenth Century
civilization can procure : I have wealth, lei-
sure, position, consideration ; all the pleasantness of large fortune and high station are
mine. Well and good. Then, suddenly,
presto ! I am deprived of all this. I
find myself stripped, as it were, and sent
naked into the world. For one, two, three,
five, six years, I am constrained to live the
life of an outlaw, an exile, a pauper, a Bohemian, a social nonentity. But do you imagine
that I resign myself to the change ? No, in-

deed, far from it. I support it as best I may, with patience, with dignity, uncomplainingly but never with resignation, until my hopes of regaining my rights become realizable, and I see then, so to speak, I see reinstatement and restoration, within arm's reach. I see myself returned to my own country, my own house, my home, my books, my properties ; I see myself re-established in my natural position among men, surrounded again by my friends, waited on by my servants, universally honoured and respected ; I see all this within arm's reach ; but then . . . ? What then ? Lo! I find myself brought face to face with a new obstacle, the obstacle I had least foreseen : nothing less than the opposition of my daughter, of my own flesh and blood, *parbleu!* She would have me throw my opportunity out of the window, and voluntarily continue this dog's life. The viper that I have warmed in my bosom turns and stings me. Thoughtless, ungrateful, unnatural child !'

'Yes, yes, you are quite right,' I confessed, between my sobs. 'I did not realize what I said. You forgive me ? Oh, you must forgive me. I would never really oppose myself to anything that was for your good. It was just the feeling of the moment. The idea of a complete alteration in our life frightened me. And Prince Léonticheff, . . . there is something about him that frightens me too, and makes me feel uncomfortable. But of course, you are right, and I was altogether wrong. Say that you forgive me. Won't you say it ? Oh, if you are going to be angry with me, and not love me, what shall I do? You are all I have in the world. Oh, I am so lonesome, so unhappy !'

'Why, I believe you are hysterical,' said my father. 'There! Stop your crying. Dry your eyes. Love you ? What a question

to ask me! I should think you would know
that my love for you is the ruling passion of
my life. There, there, my dear! You see
it is telling upon you, as well as upon me,
this life of hardship and privation. It is
consuming away your youth, it is wearing
you out. It is ageing you before your time.
You have not been yourself for these many
weeks. You are losing your colour, your
freshness, your vivacity. The new life, the
life of ease and luxury, that is about to open
before us, will be as much to your benefit as
to mine. Now go to bed, and sleep. Good-
night.'

IV.

My conception of the character of Prince Léonticheff was a good deal complicated and confused by my reading of the manuscript novel that he had left with me. I could not quite agree with him in regarding it as the most poetical thing in English prose, 'or in German, either'; nor could I share his belief that Goethe would have given all he ever wrote for the central idea or theme. But, nevertheless, it struck me as an exceedingly pretty story, extremely well wrought out. It was graceful and delicate in form, tender and refined in feeling, original in plan, and thoroughly interesting. It seemed to me to

reveal a fine imagination, a peculiarly genuine
insight into human nature, and a point of
view that was at once lofty and enlightened.
That absence of humour which was so
grotesquely distinctive of the author's personality, I did not feel in his work : perhaps
because the story he had to tell,—a tragical
romance of the middle ages,—was not one
that called for humorous treatment.

How Prince Léonticheff could ever have
written it, was the problem that baffled me.
Suppose I had discovered a cabbage-stalk
bearing lilies of the valley ? Before I had
read his novel, I should have said, if anybody
had asked me to describe him, ' He is, for
all his noble pedigree, a big, lazy, heavy
Russian mouzhik. He is well-informed upon
certain subjects, he is shrewd, he has plenty
of rough and ready mother-wit; but he is
vulgar, vain, and boastful to a degree that
would seem to indicate some congenital

weakness in his brain ; he is intolerably
wearisome ; and he is absolutely deficient
in imagination, in sensibility, in tact and
delicacy, in all those faculties and instincts
which are called æsthetic. He is the bull in
the china-shop, but a good-natured bull, it
must be confessed.'

What, however, could I say of him
now ?

It was as if the bull had suddenly dis-
played an ability to sing like a nightingale.
All my calculations were upset.

My father said, ' The rough cloak has a
silken lining.'

' Bah-bah !' cried Armidis. ' He hires
some poor devil of a clever fellow to write
for him ; then he signs the product with his
princely name, and reaps the glory of it.
Don't tell *me* !'

Armidis, I thought, was perversely unjust
to the Prince. He had made up his mind

to see nothing good in him, to believe nothing but evil of him.

I accepted my father's metaphor, and said with him, 'The rough cloak has a silken lining.'

We saw the Prince every day. He was always calling upon us at our hotel, having us to lunch with him, to dine with him, taking us to drive, sending us handsomely bound copies of his works, sending us wines, fruits, and big baskets of flowers that looked queer and out of place in our small dingy quarters. If he had sent us cut flowers, it would have been different; but the vast, stiff, conventional baskets that he did send, made my father's little room resemble the *loge* of a prima-donna.

For my part, I found his constant and profuse attentions inexplicable as well as embarrassing. Why should he neglect all the other people he knew in Paris, to devote

himself exclusively to us ? And not to speak
of the larger service that he had undertaken
to render my father, here he was daily over-
whelming us with smaller favours for which
we were in no position to render an equivalent. I could not understand it; it troubled
me, and made me feel uncomfortable and ill
at ease.

One day Armidis said to me,—my father
had gone with his Serene Highness to some
races at Longchamps ; and the composer had
taken me to dine with him on the other side
of the river,—he said, 'I am going to talk
very seriously to you for a few minutes,
Monica Paulovna. To begin with, answer
me this : don't you think I am really the
most forbearing and long-suffering friend
that ever was ?'

'I think you are the best and dearest
friend,' I responded. 'But what do you
mean by long-suffering and forbearing ?'

'Why, the way I stick to you through,—
or, rather, in spite of,—thick and thin.'

'*Through* thick and thin, indeed. But
how in spite of?'

'Oh, dear me! You literal thing! So
dense, and so unkind! To make a man
explain his little metaphors!... Your father's
thin, isn't he? And heaven knows, your
Prince is thick.'

I could not help smiling, though I tried to
speak with great severity, when I said, 'I
have told you before, and I wish you would
remember it, that I cannot allow you to
abuse my father. As for the Prince, I am
no partisan of his, but you are utterly unjust
to him. He is a very harmless person; uncouth, uncivilized, if you please, and dread-
fully tedious; but thoroughly well-meaning
and kind-hearted. And though he says
stupid and vulgar things, he writes very well
indeed. You have taken a dislike to him, a

prejudice against him; and you are determined to believe nothing but evil of him.
It's unworthy of you.'

'Oh, dear me! What a crusher! I feel
quite blasted. You pitiless unfeeling creature!... However, I have a duty to discharge, and I'll discharge it, no matter what
it costs me. Only, please don't stare at me
in quite such a stony way. It disconcerts
me, and saps my courage.... Let me see....
Where shall I begin?'

He paused for an instant, and looked at
me with one of his bright, irresistible smiles:
a smile like that of a naughty but charming
child, eager to be taken back into your good
graces, but not by any means willing to
promise to sin no more: a smile against
which no rancour could be proof. He looked
at me thus, until he saw that my own face
was melting, whether I would or not; and
then he went on....

'There ! That is better, and so much more becoming. Now, what I am in duty bound to say to you is this: If I did not know you to be entirely incapable of such a thing, I should accuse you of carrying on the most desperate sort of a flirtation with Prince Léonticheff.'

'Mr. Armidis !' I cried, in anger and amazement.

'Oh, don't. Don't Mr. Armidis me. I haven't done anything to deserve it. I tell you in my very first breath that I know you to be incapable of such a thing. I was only warning you of what I might say if I knew you less well, of what a stranger, witnessing your attitude towards the Prince, might say, of what, in fine, the Prince himself very likely thinks. I know you're not flirting with him ; but he, I'll bet my head, believes you are. Now wait a moment. Don't fling out at me. Contain yourself, and let me explain. The

Prince, in one word, is making desperate love to you ; and you are suffering him to do so unrebuked.   The real reason is, you're so innocent and unsophisticated that you've never suspected what he was up to.   But he doesn't know that, and he naturally thinks you like it.'

'The Prince making love to me!   What an absurd idea!' I cried.

'Yes ; isn't it ?   Entirely absurd ; quite so ; preposterous.   We're altogether of one mind concerning that, I'm rejoiced to learn.   But absurd as it is, it's so.   Now listen to me. You're a woman, a young,—comparatively speaking, a young, — unmarried woman. You've had scarcely any experience of the world, and none of men.   What men have you ever known ?   Your father, Julian North, and poor old Armidis, the composer.   Well, my dear, they don't any of them count.   Each is an exception to the rules.   But your horrid

old Léonticheff! There's an average man, a
typical man. . . .'

'Prince Léonticheff a typical man !' I could
not help interrupting. 'If there ever was an
exception, it seems to me he is one.'

'Oh, for that, yes,' assented Armidis.
'Also an exception in certain little superficial
ways; but on the whole, and under his skin,
a fair average specimen of the brute beast
called man for short. An average specimen
in that he has the average passions, appetites,
weaknesses, and code of morals. Well and
good. You don't know the species; I do.
You are at a loss how to construe its actions;
to me they speak louder than words. Now
when I see an individual of the stripe of
Prince Léonticheff devoting himself to a
young and pretty woman as he's devoting
himself to Miss Banakin, I know that his
designs are not platonic. I know that he is
making love to her, with malice aforethought.

And, what is more, I know that, seeing that she doesn't resent his advances, or snub him, or put him back in his place, he believes that she likes it, and is encouraging him, leading him on, and meeting him half way. . . .'

'But he's *not* devoting himself to me,' I protested.

'Oh, he's not devoting himself to you? No? Really? Oh, then I crave a thousand pardons. I thought he was. I thought he came to see you every day, and took you driving nearly every day, and sent you flowers and books and things every other day, and was never contented unless you were dining or lunching with him, and that sort of thing. Somehow I had acquired that impression. . . .'

'It is my father. He comes to see my father,' I began. . . .

'Your father? Oh, wow-wow! Your

father's very nice, perhaps; it's a matter of taste, and perhaps he's very nice. Yes, as a famous statesman used to say, I've no doubt that for the people who like that sort of man, he'd be just about the sort of man they'd like. But somehow, as the world is constituted, young men don't conceive such insatiable passions for Fathers : no, generally daughters. And then consider! He scarcely speaks to your father. He has nor eyes, nor ears, nor tongue for anyone but you. He glues himself to you like a tame rhinoceros. Oh, believe me, I know the type. The Prince is wooing you. And he flatters himself that you encourage him. I can't altogether blame him. You pale women with the red hair are the devil and all where men's hearts are concerned. But I do blame you a little. You ought to pour some cold water down his patrician back. You ought not to let him fancy that he's made an impression. If you don't look sharp, he'll marry you. There! I have spoken.'

'No, no, you are talking nonsense,' I rejoined. 'Prince Léonticheff has never said or done or hinted anything in the least degree sentimental. If he seems devoted, it's only his way; it doesn't mean anything at all. I will confess to you that I do not relish his attentions. They embarrass me horribly, and make me feel uncomfortable and disagreeable. The books, the flowers, the dinners, the drives, the constant visits, his general eagerness to please us, to serve us, they make me squirm; I wish he would stop. But what can I do? I mustn't offend him. For my father's sake, I mustn't offend him. What can I do? What would you have me do?'

'Well, I don't know, I'm sure. I'm not a woman. I can warn you, I can put you on your guard; but I can't tell you how to

defend yourself. That's a woman's business.
I thought I had read somewhere, or heard a
rumour, to the effect that women generally
know without being taught how to assert
their dignity, and put a too presuming suitor
back into his place. I thought women knew
how to do this by a sort of instinct. I
thought they had a method all their own by
which, quietly, gracefully, with an air of
unconsciousness, to wrap round a man a
beautiful, filmy, delicate, but very cold wet
blanket. Search within thyself. All I can
say is that your horrid old Russian Prince
has designs upon you. If they are not
honourable designs, which is entirely
possible, *je m'en fiche !* In that case, I
know he is in no wise to be feared. Only I
should like to see you shrivel him up with
your scorn. But if his designs *are*
honourable, which somehow seems most
likely,—why, then, I tremble. Your dear

delightful papa's little ambition will be realized; and heaven pity Monica Paulovna.'

'My father's ambition? What do you mean?'

'Oh, nothing to speak of. Your father's ambition is simple, natural, and unpretentious. He aspires to marry you to the Prince.'

'Oh, that is too absurd!'

'All the same, it is the fact.'

'Never, never. My father's not a fool. He knows in the first place that I will never marry anyone. In the second place, he can see with his eyes shut that no two people could possibly be more unsuited to each other than Prince Léonticheff and I. And in the third place, he knows that a Prince of the Empire isn't likely to ask me to be his wife. He can pretend to the highest.'

'Even so! Your father's not a fool. Therefore he sees, as I do, that your prince is tremendously smitten by your charms ; he realizes that from a worldly point of view such a marriage would be immensely brilliant and advantageous : wealth, rank, a title, position, power, everything that a worldling's heart can desire, at one fell swoop! And if you were not related to him, I should tell you that your dear papa is very far from being above worldly considerations. Nothing this side of Paradise could give him such joyous satisfaction as an alliance between his daughter and the Prince Léonticheff. As for Julian, poor lad, whom I fancy you had in mind when you said you wouldn't marry anyone, your father regards him as quite out of the running. Indeed, he never regarded him as in it ; and if he was suave and amiable in dealing with him, it was only to get rid of him the more easily. Nothing that your father ever did increased my appreciation of the solid diplomatic worth

that lies under the surface of his guileless-
seeming character, as did the adroit and
noiseless manner in which he sent Julian
North packing off into the wilderness. Let
the Prince once declare his intentions, and
then watch Paul the son of Michael. The
worst of it is, I am afraid you will be weak
and obedient.'

'You needn't be afraid of that, if it ever
comes to the point. I did not know you had
so poor an opinion of me.'

'Well, we'll see, we'll see. Don't boast; it
brings bad luck. Your father has charms to
move the filial breast. He's not a man to
stick at a trifle, and neither is your prince.
If they conspire together to make a bride of
you,—beware, beware! I wish to speak
moderately, without passion, without prejudice, and therefore I will say nothing more
disparaging of Prince Léonticheff than that
he is the most colossal mass of swinish

selfishness that I could ever have imagined possible in my worst nightmares. So long as his appetites are satisfied, he smiles and is content. But heaven help the man, woman, or child, that stands between him and the object his mouth waters for! You might as reasonably look for mercy from a hungry tiger,—courtesy from an anaconda,—compunction from an escaped locomotive.'

' Prince Léonticheff is not one hundredth part so black as you paint him. I am not by any means his champion or admirer, but I can't understand why you should be so persistently unjust to him.'

' Unjust, say you? Now, look you, Monica Banakin, I will endure well-nigh anything from you, because I love you. But I will not endure to hear you call me unjust on the score of your Russian Prince. Anything but that. I have had opportunities of judging him which have been denied to you. I have spent several unhappy hours quite alone with him, *en tête-à-tête*, listening to his free and guileless prattle. I have heard him deliver his mind on various themes, human and otherwise, with a degree of candour and unreserve which even he could scarcely employ in the presence of a young unmarried woman. Now, then, I maintain that I am not merely just, but that I temper justice with mercy, when I call Prince Léonticheff the most appalling monster of gross egotism that I have ever encountered. I maintain that I speak with gratuitous temperance when I allude to him as the most odious cad that has ever entered my horizon. Far be it from me to blacken his fair fame; therefore I will say nothing further, except that in his conversation, and, by his own accounts, in his life as well, he is an indecent beast. If you ask me to classify him zoologically, I will add that he seems to me a cross between

a boa-constrictor and a pig. You see, I hold
myself within bounds. There is no villainy,
no cruelty, no bestiality of which he would
be incapable, if it suited his desire....
Now, my dear, I want you to snub him.
Do it gently, do it discreetly, but do it
firmly. Put him back in his place, and let
him stay there. That's all. I have said my
little say. Now let's banish him from our
thoughts. He takes away my appetite, and
his name in my mouth tastes bitter.'

Was Prince Léonticheff so bad as Armidis
pretended? I could not believe it. The
very excess of superlatives with which
Armidis loaded him, shook my confidence in
the speaker's judgment.

As for his suggestion that the Prince
wanted to marry me, it was too utterly
absurd to deserve a second thought.

V.

It was too utterly absurd to deserve a second thought; and yet...

And yet, within a six-month, I became the Princess Léonticheff.

I must explain, if I can, how step by step I was brought to do so. I say, ' If I can,' because, when I think of it now, it seems so inexplicable to me, so contrary to all natural-ness and verisimilitude, that I should declare it to be impossible, the shadow of a bad dream, if I did not, unhappily, know it to be a most substantial fact.

Armidis had said, ' If you don't look sharp, he'll marry you.'

To which I had responded, 'Nonsense!
He has never said or done or hinted anything in the least degree sentimental.'

The next day he asked me to be his wife.

Towards five o'clock in the afternoon he
called upon us, and announced that he had
come to take me off for a drive.

'Your father permits. I want to talk to
you about something important. Go make
ready.'

I would much rather have stayed at home.
In the first place, the prospect of a long
tête-à-tête with him looked wearisome and
uninviting. In the second place, though I
did not believe that Armidis's assertions
of yesterday rested upon the slightest
foundation of truth, they had had, nevertheless, the effect of making me feel
conscious and ill at ease in Prince
Léonticheff's presence, and I did not care to
be alone with him. Yet, on the other hand,

if I should refuse to go, he might take it amiss; whereas, for my father's sake, I must avoid unnecessarily offending him. And then, perhaps, the 'something important' concerning which he wished to speak with me, was some aspect of my father's affair which he could not mention in my father's presence.

This last consideration played the chief part in determining me. I went to my room, and put on my hat and gloves.

The Prince's Victoria was in waiting in the street.

'Well,' said the Prince, as soon as we were fairly off, 'I've had news from Russia.'

He paused. I did not speak, but waited expectantly for his next word.

'Do you mind my smoking a cigarette? Thank you... Yes, I've had news from Russia; and, not to beat about the bush, bad news at that.'

He paused again ; and I, feeling that some response was expected from me, repeated, ' Bad news . . . ?' with a suspension of the voice that meant, ' Yes. Go on. Tell me, quick.'

' I thought,' he went on, ' that I would confide it to you in the first place, and then afterwards break it to your father. Poor old chap, he's worked himself up to such a pitch of hopeful excitement, a set-back now might play the devil with him.'

' Yes.   That   was   very   considerate   of you.'

' Oh, not at all, You see, I felt that it might make him downright ill.   Besides, after you and I have had a talk together, perhaps the whole complexion of the news may be changed.   We may be able between us to extract the venom from it.'

Would he never come to his point ? ' The news is . . . ?' I questioned.

'Well, here... I don't remember whether I told you that I had written to a friend of mine at St. Petersburg,—a man who stands wonderfully near the throne,—that I had written to him to find out whether or not the Emperor had any personal feeling against your father. It was of the highest importance for me to be informed as to that. It would determine, so to speak, my method of attack. If he had no knowledge of the affair, or feeling in regard to it, except officially, then I would go to work in one way. If on the other hand he felt in any degree personally aggrieved against the old boy,—why, then, naturally, my tactics would be entirely different.'

'Yes, I remember, you told me you had written. And now you have had an answer from your friend?'

'Exactly. I got a letter from him this morning. And to cut a long story short, he

says that, as ill luck will have it, the
Emperor bears the strongest sense of
personal injury. It appears that, when, soon
after his accession, your father's partisans
brought his case to the Emperor's notice,
and began to plead with him for a pardon,
he, like the sensible man he is, asked to see
the documents bearing upon the matter ; and
the manuscripts found in your father's possession were handed to him ; and he read
them. Now, I don't want to cast any re-
flection upon your father. I like him, and
I esteem him as a man with a certain sort of
intelligence. But you must allow me to say
that in some respects he's little better than a
fool. Fancy, if you please, that among these
manuscripts there was one, written,—as, for
the matter of that, they all were,—at a
time when Alexander III. was still the
Tsesarevitch, which consisted of a series of
not very flattering predictions as to what

policy he would probably pursue upon
coming to the throne ; and his Majesty read
that, and it didn't please him. What under
God's heaven ever induced your father to
write it, is more than I can tell. It was
as needless and as purposeless as it was
dangerous and idiotic. But there it lay in
black and white, all nicely dated, and signed
with your father's name. His Majesty read
it, and he didn't like it. And, weary of the
importunities of your father's friends, he
dropped a hint that he would make it
uncommonly disagreeable for any person
who might thereafter mention Paul Mikhaelovitch Banakin's name in his presence. " I
must live up to the reputation he has given
me," was his imperial little *mot*. And my
correspondent adds that it would be highly
imprudent even for me to seek to approach
him on the subject; that I would run a
considerable risk of getting into his bad

books, and losing my standing and favour at
the Court.'

The Prince turned his broad red face full
upon me, and closed one eye, and smiled.

' Then,' said I,—and I was conscious of a
strange and altogether unjustifiable sense of
relief,—' then it is a hopeless case? My
father's affairs will have to remain as they
are ?'

' Not so fast, not so fast,' returned the
Prince. ' I didn't say it was a hopeless case.
What can't be done by hook, can perhaps be
done by crook. In fact, to put the long and
the short of the matter in five words, from
this moment the success or failure of the
whole enterprise depends solely upon you.'

' Upon me ?'

' Quite so. Upon you.'

' But how ? I don't see how. What can
I do ?'

' That's just what I am going to tell you.

It was to tell you that, that I asked you out
to drive with me. Well, it's this way. If I
approach the Emperor on the subject of
your father's wrongs, says my friend, I run
the risk of angering him, and of losing my
standing and favour at Court. Well, that's a
pretty big, a pretty serious risk to run, isn't
it? Rather, you say. And if you know
anything about human nature, you know that
a man in his senses isn't likely to run a risk
of that sort, unless there's a prize at the
other end of it. A sane man isn't going to
run a risk like that out of pure benevolence.
Now, I'm a wonderfully good-natured fellow,
as you must have seen ; and I'd do a good
deal, and risk a good deal, just from sheer
kindness of heart. But not my standing and
favour with the Father of his People. I
stop just short of that. That is too precious
to me. Considerably more than half of my
influence and usefulness in this world springs

from that. I can't risk it, except for the chance of a big reward. Now, then, my dear Mademoiselle, it's for you to guarantee me my reward.'

For me to guarantee him his reward!

Suddenly I grew cold to the very marrow of my bones ; and a tremor of fear and nervousness seized upon me. I turned my face from the Prince, and looked into the street from the other side of the carriage. Oh, if I could only escape, and get away from him, out of his sight, beyond the sound of his voice, alone, anywhere, to avoid what I doubted not was coming ! That was the only thought or feeling that would take shape in my mind.

'You see what I mean,' he went on. 'You must promise to marry me. I consider that an adequate *quid pro quo.* You betroth yourself to me. Then I make a little run into Russia, and obtain an audience of the

Emperor, and brave his wrath, and plead
your father's cause. I believe I shall not
plead in vain. It may be hard work, a pull
against the tide, and all that. But I think I
can assure you that I will not come away till
I have got an imperial pardon for the old
boy in my pocket. At the same time I will
crave his majesty's sanction for our marriage.
I dare say I have told you that I make it a
practice never to fail in anything that I
seriously undertake. There, now; I expect
you to consider yourself from this hour my
fiancée ... What have you to answer ?'

What had I to answer! My thoughts
were in such turmoil and confusion, I could
not find words for my answer, the only
answer that I had to make. And even if the
words had come to me, my heart was
beating so hard, I doubt if I could have
spoken them. All at once a fierce hatred of
the Prince had seemed to grow big, and

burn within me; a hot, savage anger. Oh,
if I could only jump from the carriage, and
run away, and never see his face, nor hear
his voice, again so long as I lived! I kept
my back turned towards him, and bit my
lips, and was speechless. I remembered
what Armidis had said, that women generally
knew by instinct how to silence an unwelcome suitor; and I wondered bitterly why
that instinct was denied to me.

'Yes,' the Prince continued, in his fat,
complacent manner, 'you and I must become
engaged. You say you don't love me. I
know you say that, though you don't open
your lips, because you're a young girl, and
all young girls have romantic and sentimental
ideas about love and marriage. You say
you don't love me; but the important
question is, What do I say? I say, Never
mind. I say also that it is only a question of
time when you will love me. I never yet

knew,—this is strictly between ourselves,—I
never yet knew a woman who could help
loving me, if I seriously tried to make her.
And, — again between you and me, — I
suppose I've made love to, and been loved
by, something like two hundred women in
the last ten years. Yes, two hundred would
be a moderate estimate, a very moderate
estimate indeed. All sorts and conditions of
women, too, mind you ; from all ranks of
life ; of all ages between eighteen and thirty-
five ; of pretty nearly all nationalities,—
French and English, Russian and German,
Italian and Spanish, even Turkish women,
Greeks, and Jewesses. Oh, but not with a
view to matrimony ; no, no, no. You're the
one single woman on the face of this planet
whom I have looked at with the idea of
inviting her to become my wife. You say
you don't love me ; and I say never mind,
for the present. Love isn't necessary to

begin a marriage with. The necessary
capital to begin with is respect and liking.
Now, I'm quite sure that you respect me and
like me. You can't help doing so, because
you're a fair-minded, sensible woman, and
I'm a thoroughly likeable man, and
thoroughly worthy of respect. Very good ;
you marry me with your respect and liking
as a basis. If I'm satisfied, I don't see that
anybody else is called upon to complain.
As for love, that will come ; you may safely
leave that to me. For my own part, I not
only respect and like you, but I am free to
say that I've conceived for you the most
violent passion that I have ever felt for any
woman in my life. And from the first day I
saw you here in Paris, a few weeks ago, I
confess, I've realized that you were the
woman designed by heaven to be my wife.
My wife has got to be, first of all, a Russian ;
and you're a Russian. Then she's got to be

noble, and you belong to one of the oldest noble families in the Empire. You might expect me to say that she's got to be rich, too; but I'm rich enough myself to dispense with a *dot* from my bride, if I choose. Then she's got to be pretty; and to say no more, your appearance and style suit me better than those of any other woman I've ever seen. Finally she's got to be clever and intellectual; and you're that, beyond any sort of question. So! I've thought it all over carefully and from every point of view; and I've decided to make you the Princess Léonticheff. You may take that as a great tribute to your charms, in more ways than one. Not to mention the magnificent rank to which I offer to raise you, you must understand that I'm a very difficult and critical man, extremely hard to please. What's more, until I saw you, I had always said I shouldn't even think of marriage till I was past forty. But directly I did see you, it was all up with me. You took me captive at once... I'm going to speak to your father about it as soon as we return from this drive. I tell you, you will wear your new dignity like one to the manner born! I can just see you,—Madame la Princesse, ruling it over Salchester House, wearing the Léonticheff jewels, surrounded by admiring people, a very Queen, by Jove! You were born for luxury, and I'm going to give it to you. You can't imagine how proud of you I'll be! What with your own natural beauty, and the sumptuous setting I'll provide for it, the people will turn and stare at you wherever you go; and how they'll envy me!'

Was ever woman in this humour wooed?

At last I found my voice, though it was a weak voice and tremulous, I am afraid.

'I assure you, Prince Léonticheff,' I said,

'that I can never under any circumstances become your wife. Will you—will you be good enough to tell your coachman to drive home?'

'Of course,' he rejoined composedly, 'it strikes you as unlikely, even as impossible, at a first glance. But when you come to think it over, you'll conclude that it's not only possible, it's inevitable. I myself, I don't mind owning, when the idea first occurred to me, I scouted it as absurd. "Pshaw!" I said. "You don't want to get married, my good fellow. You don't want to sacrifice all the independence and irresponsibility of bachelorhood, just for the sake of calling a pretty woman by your name. Nonsense!" But gradually the idea grew upon me, grew upon me; and by-and-by I woke up to recognise it as a case of willy-nilly. You've inspired me with a passion so deep and violent that I shan't know any sort

of peace till I've made you my own; and
I've got too much respect both for you and
your father to look at you with any idea in
my head save that of honourable matrimony.
You've taken such a hold upon my heart
and upon my imagination that I can't think
or dream of anything else.   It surprises
you perhaps; but it can't begin to surprise
you as it surprises me.   I never would have
believed that I was capable of such a terribly
serious attachment.   I've had so many little
unmeaning fancies and amourettes, that I
had rather come to regard myself as proof
against anything more fatal.   But here I
am, completely undone and knocked under
by your loveliness.   You see, there's no
escaping it.   We'll have to get married.
I'll make a formal demand for your hand of
your father when we return to the Hôtel du
St.-Esprit.   Now, if you like, we may change
the subject.'

'I wish to tell you, Prince Léonticheff,' I
said, 'although you do not appear to pay
any attention to what I tell you, that I will
never become your wife. Nothing that you
can say or do, nothing that anybody can say
or do, nothing that can possibly happen,
can ever induce me to become your wife.
Nothing. I beg of you to accept that as
my final answer. I must also beg you never
to speak to me of this again, and not to
speak of it to my father. It will do no good
for you to speak of it to him ; it will only
bring trouble to him and me, without at all
altering my resolution ; it will only bring
trouble and struggle. You have spoken to
me to-day in a very unusual way; you
have said things to me that most women
would find intolerably offensive and insulting.
But in spite of all that, I still believe you
to be a man of kind natural feelings, and
that you are only lacking in tact and ima-

gination. If you do not wish me to think worse of you, you will obey my wishes in this respect, without my saying anything more.'

'That illustrates perfectly the point that I was making. It will take you some time to accustom yourself to the idea. At first it seems impossible to you ; and it frets you, it disturbs you. As for my being a man of kind feelings, of course I am. I am the kindest man you know, and the best friend you've got in the world. You can see for yourself how anxious I am to serve you, you and your father. And if you consider it insulting for me to speak of a *quid pro quo* —why, look here. You can't expect a man to put his head into the lion's mouth, so to speak, for mere acquaintance' sake, can you ? You can hardly expect me to run the risk of disgracing myself at Court out of pure abstract altruism. But for my future wife,

and my future father-in-law—ah, that's a
very different matter. You see, I hate cant,
and I talk to you with a degree of honesty
that may seem brutal, but which is natural
and proper. For the rest, I leave you to
perceive unaided how in every way this offer
of marriage from me to you is to your advantage. I am a modest man, and I shan't
dwell on that. Anyhow, it's too obvious;
to do so would be to insult your intelligence.
I will only say that there is no unmarried
woman in Europe, under the blood-royal,
who wouldn't jump at a chance to become
the Princess Léonticheff, and I may add that
an alliance with royalty itself wouldn't be too
high a thing for me to look to, if I cared
for it. I'm no mere puny Russian Prince,
you must remember; I'm a Prince of the
Empire. I'm one of the richest men in
Europe, at the same time, and one of the
ablest writers. Why, if I ask a woman to

marry me, she ought to go about all the rest
of her mortal days thanking her stars for her
luck. It isn't conceivable that any woman
in cold blood should refuse me. Why, if I
told you the names of some of the families
in Russia, in England, in Prussia, in France,
that have flung their daughters at my head,
you'd be amazed, you could hardly credit it.
I'm his Serene Highness Prince Léonticheff;
don't allow yourself to forget that. ... It
may not be so clear to you how the union
I propose will be equally to my advantage,
but that's only because you don't understand
yet how fond I am of you. My heart is set
upon you, and when my heart is set upon
a thing I must have it. Yes, the thing is
inevitable, it's bound to be. You must make
up your mind to it. You must think it over,
and try to realize the grand good fortune
that has happened to you. All unmarried
Europe will envy you. But apart from that,

you're not going to set yourself up as the single obstacle between your father and his chances of restoration to his rights in Russia ; you couldn't find it in you to do that. And I—I'm not going to let you, the prettiest and the sweetest woman I've ever known, and the woman I've fallen desperately in love with, I'm not going to let you continue to slave your youth away as a music-teaching drudge here in Paris. It isn't right; it must be stopped; it's gone on six years too long already. Your father tells me, and I'm able to see for myself, that it's gradually wearing you out. Your strength is failing you. Why, he says, you've grown visibly thin and pallid even during the last few months. He's very seriously alarmed about you ; and if you were wise, you'd be alarmed about yourself. Suppose your health should give out ? Here you are, so

to speak, the sole prop your poor old father
has to lean upon, his breadwinner, his nurse,
his comforter. Well, suppose your health
should break down ? Eh ? Where would
he be ? And if you have to go on drudging
and worrying very much longer, your health
will break down, and then there'll be the
devil to pay. No; what you must do is
written upon the walls; marry Prince Gigi.
Then your father will be re-established in
the possession of his own properties; and
you'll have a rich husband to take care of
you, and protect you from all harm. That's
my last word for the present. It is understood that you and I are engaged.'

'Prince Léonticheff, will you be so good
as to tell your coachman to drive home ?' I
demanded.

'Stonehouse !' he called out. 'Back to the
Rue St.-Jacques.'

We finished our drive in silence. To me it seemed to last hours and hours. When it was over I went straight to my room, leaving Prince Léonticheff to join my father in his.

VI.

I WENT straight to my room, and locked my door behind me.

Exhausted, unnerved, unstrung, I flung myself upon my bed, and closed my eyes. In my weakness, I could not shake off a feeling like terror, as if I were in some immediate, imminent peril. I could not shake it off, though I knew perfectly well that it was unreasonable and groundless; and it afforded me a sense of security and relief to think that my door was locked.

Never to see Prince Léonticheff again! Never again to hear his voice, feel his presence! I was surfeited with him. The

mere thought of him filled me with sickening
disgust. I remember I said to myself, ' I
will not leave this room until I can do so
without the slightest risk of having to meet
him. No, not until I know that he has gone
away from Paris.' It did not occur to me
how difficult, how impossible, of performance
this vow might prove to be. It struck me
as the simplest, the easiest, thing in the
world, just to shut myself up in my room,
and refuse to open my door, until I was
persuaded that Prince Léonticheff had gone
away from Paris.

And then—my father! I was oppressed
by a great weary dread of the struggle which
I knew I should presently have to undertake
and carry on with my father. I had told the
Prince that I would never become his wife,
that nothing conceivable could ever induce
me to become his wife ; and it had been,
comparatively speaking, easy for me to say

that to him. But I knew that I should presently have to repeat it to my father, to repeat it and maintain it; and from that prospect I shrank fatigued beforehand, as from a labour far beyond my strength.

I did not see my father again that evening. He came to my door, it is true, and rapped, and said it was time to go to dinner.

'We have been waiting for you. Why do you delay? Make haste.'

But I answered that I had a headache, and was tired, and did not want any dinner; and rather to my surprise, and very much to my relief, he went away without insisting.

In the morning, however, I said to myself, 'What must be must be. I have got to have it out with him sooner or later. Nothing can be gained by putting it off. On the contrary, it is best to nip the thing in its bud. They can't make me marry him by main force. This notion of staying in my room is quite impracticable: I have things to do. Besides, it would give the affair too much importance; it would be a confession of weakness and of fear of them. I must put on a bold front, I must seem absolutely determined, and absolutely confident of my own strength. Come!'

So I plucked up my courage, and went down to my father's room. My teeth were set, and my fingers were clenched, but my heart was beating so hard that it pained me.

My father greeted me kindly, and with a certain air of gay raillery.

'Ah, *ma fille!*' he cried, patting my cheek, and laughing into my eyes. 'Our headache is better? We have slept it off? *Allons! Pas de mauvaise honte!* Confess! It was but a little ruse, a little innocent, transparent ruse, whereby to hide our blushes? Eh? Eh?'

He paused, and looked at me with a face

all smiles. Then he made a bow, and said,
' But I forget my duties. Princess, receive
my felicitations.'

I stood still, and summoned all my self-
command, and asked, ' Prince Léonticheff
has told you what he said to me yesterday ?'
But my voice trembled, and betrayed my
nervousness.

' Naturally ! He could scarcely have done
less. And why otherwise should I offer you
my felicitations ? . . . Ah, Monica, in my
wildest dreams I have never dared to hope for
you anything approaching in brilliancy this
destiny that has actually laid itself at your
feet. You are indeed a charming girl, and
now your charms have made your fortune
for you, and mine for me. And wasn't it
a lucky day for us when I read Léonticheff's
name in *Figaro ?* Madame la Princesse !
Indeed, you deserve it, my dear, you are in
every way worthy of it. It is heaven's

compensation to you, to us, for all that we
have been called upon to suffer during the
last six years.'

'But I should suppose that he must also
have told you of the answer that I gave him,'
I said coldly.

'*Olàlà !* That doesn't matter. Piff-paff!
Whatever you may have answered on the
spur of the moment, in the flush of your
emotion and surprise, is of no consequence.
To an offer such as his there is of course
but one final answer. A Princess of the
Empire! It simply overwhelms me. I
know not how to express my joy and my
gratitude.'

'Well, father, I only wish to repeat to you
what I said to the Prince. The answer I
made on the spur of the moment will be
my final answer. I will never marry him,
never. Nothing in the world can ever
bring me to marry him. Absolutely nothing.

There is no man living whom I would not rather marry, if I had to marry at all. I wish to say this to you now, at the very beginning, so that you may understand it, and not get your heart set on the impossible, and so store up a disappointment for yourself. I will never under any conceivable circumstances marry him. It will be absolutely useless for you to try to persuade me. There is nothing imaginable that I would not rather do. I would far rather, far rather, die. If there were no other way of escaping him, I would kill myself without a moment's hesitation. But there is no danger of its coming to that. I simply will never consent to be his wife; and even if he could drag me by force to the altar, no priest will marry a woman without her consent. That is all. I feel that it is my duty to warn you of that at the very outset.'

My father looked at me with a tolerant,

incredulous smile : such a smile as one might
wear in listening to the boasting of some
silly child.   In the end he gave a gentle
little laugh.

'Poh, poh, poh!' he cried cheerfully, with
a jaunty shrug and gesture. 'Say what you
please, my dear ; I allow you complete
freedom of speech, so long as you don't let
it affect your behaviour.   Say what you
please ; but you are not an imbecile, and
I am quite sure you will do the proper
thing.   You have very good brains in your
little head, and a very good heart in your
little bosom, though sometimes you make
very foolish and very naughty speeches.'

'Well, I have said all I had to say,' I
repeated.   'I   will   never   marry   Prince
Léonticheff.   I have given you fair warning.
It is for you to accept it in your own good
time.'

'No, you are neither an imbecile, nor—

nor a little selfish cat. It would be the part
of an imbecile to let pass this most dazzling
opportunity. But it would be the part of a
black-hearted, cold-blooded egoist to stand
between her father and the realization of
his most cherished wish—to constitute herself the sole obstacle to his receiving his
rights at the hands of justice. Léonticheff
is one of the richest, one of the most illustrious, and one of the most powerful
members of the noblesse of Europe; at the
same time he is a man of the kindest and
most chivalrous nature, a man of intellect,
and a man precisely suited to you in point
of years. You are not such a fool as to
throw away a chance to unite yourself in
marriage to a man like that. It is the sort
of chance that comes but to one woman in
a million once in a generation. But, what
is more, you are aware that my hopes of
restoration to my rights in Russia all depend

upon your betrothing yourself to him. You, my daughter, my own flesh and blood, are not going to set yourself up as the sole impediment to my success? You are not so abominably selfish and ungrateful as that.'

'Yes, I know that the Prince would like me to be the price of his services to you. He was frank enough to tell me so. He said that he would consider me an adequate *quid pro quo*. I appreciate the compliment; but thank you, no!'

'What an unworthy speech! So to misrepresent the motives and intentions of a most honourable gentleman! Can't you see that it was a piece of gratuitous delicacy on his part, knowing that the marriage he proposed was one that would be entirely to our advantage, to put it as if it would be his reward for services rendered to me? And, at all events, what claims have we upon

him ? What right have we to expect him
to render us so great a service, at the risk
of what is more precious to him than his
fortune, without the promise of a reward ?
The Prince, as you say, was frank, where
other men would have been hypocritical.
All the more to his credit is it.'

'Very good. I do not wish to discuss it
with you. I may be both an imbecile and
an egoist; but one thing is very certain : I
will never marry Prince Léonticheff. A
gentleman, indeed ! It will be utterly vain
for you to talk to me about it. You can't
shake my resolution. You can only tire
yourself and me. That is all.'

VII.

THAT was late in June. In September we were formally affianced. In December we were married.

Meanwhile . . .

Armidis said to me, 'I can't bear a man who crows, you know. It's so indelicate and vulgar — in a word, Léonticheffian. But really now, am I not quite remarkable as an amateur prophet ?'

'Yes,' I admitted, laughing. 'If it gives you any satisfaction to think so, you are really quite remarkable as an amateur prophet.'

'And you own now that my estimate of the Prince's character erred, if it erred at all, on

the side of kindness ?   It's quite wonderful,
my insight into human nature.   I don't know
whether I ought to congratulate myself upon
it or not.   It is often a source of pain to be
too clear-sighted.'

'Oh, no, I don't think the Prince is
altogether the abandoned ruffian that you
would make him out.   I am not going to
marry him, and I don't like him.   I am sick
of him, his voice, his face, his vast loose
figure, his fatuous, unctuous manner, his
boastfulness, his indelicacy and indiscretion—
everything—they irk me and irritate me, and
make me squirm ; I am satiated with them.
But that is no reason why I should be unjust
to him.   I think, with all his faults, he is
well-meaning and honest according to his
light.   I think he is far more a fool than a
knave.   I don't believe he would ever do
anything if he thought it wrong.   I believe
the whole trouble with him is a lack of

humour. He has no perspective, no sense of congruity. That accounts for his grossest solecisms, his enormous self-conceit, his brutality and obstinacy, all his unpleasant traits. But I am sure that he is really, down deep, kind-hearted and well-meaning. A thoroughly bad man never could have written *Drachensnest.*'

'Oh, dear! What a dangerous state of mind! Oh, if you go on believing that there is a single microscopical particle of good in him, they'll have you married to him yet. Oh, for my sake, won't you please think that he is just the most hopelessly immoral scoundrel that was ever created, and the most egregious cad, and the most fatuous idiot? You might think that, to oblige a friend.'

'I should be glad to oblige you; but I don't see how I can force myself to think what isn't so.'

'Then I tremble for you. Beware, beware !'

My father, at first, would not pay the least attention to my refusal, would not take it with any degree of seriousness.

'I do not scold you, I do not reason with you, nor plead with you,' he said. 'Why? Are you curious to learn why? Well, simply because I consider you already betrothed to the Prince. Remember, you are his promised bride.'

The Prince himself pretended to assume the same attitude. 'We are engaged to be married, you know,' he would remind me from time to time.

I, for the most part, kept silence.

My father demanded, 'How long do you intend to pout and sulk, like a silly child? How long before you are going to behave reasonably, like a full-grown woman? How long before you will accept the good fortune that heaven has sent you, and be thankful for it ?'

I did not answer; but I wondered, ' How long before they will realize the utter futility of their conduct ?'

One day—the Prince having repeated for perhaps the fiftieth time, ' We are engaged, you know '—I asked him, ' If that is so, why do you loiter here in Paris ? Why don't you keep your promise, perform your part of the agreement, go to Russia, and obtain a pardon for my father from your friend the Tsar ?'

' Ah, but... !' he cried.

'Am I to consider that a sufficient answer ?' I inquired.

' But, don't you see, it's this way. I fancy I would prefer to wait about doing that until our engagement is sealed and ratified by your own word of assent. It's only a formality, of course, like the Queen's signature to a law in England ; yet I think I will wait till it is complied with. I'm a wonderfully patient man.'

'Oh, then,' said I, 'I suspect that our engagement is not such an absolutely certain thing after all.'

'On the contrary, quite certain, positively certain,' he retorted. 'Only I am like these Parisian cabbies, *je demande des arrhes !*'

Armidis told me one day that he had had 'such a pathetic little confidence' from my father.

'Such a pathetic little confidence, poor dear man! He complains that you do nothing but pout and sulk. He can't get a word from you; nothing but just pouting, sulking silence. He wouldn't mind it so much, he says, except that he fears it may end by antagonizing the Prince. He's afraid his Serene Highness will get tired and go away . . . A word to the wise, my dear!

Continue to pout and sulk and hold your
pretty tongue.'

Presently my father began to lose patience.
He began to argue with me. He reminded
me that it was the invariable custom among
people of our class and nation for young girls
to marry the husbands whom their parents,
from the vantage ground of greater age,
experience, and wisdom, picked out for them.

'We are not Americans,' he said. 'We
are not Gypsies or Bohemians. We are
Russians, and we are noble, of the superior
nobility. Has any woman of your family, or
of your class, ever dreamed of contracting a
marriage except at the will of her parents?
Or ever dreamed of rejecting the man of her
parents' selection? Why should you, by
what right do you, expect to be an exception
to the rule? The trouble is that, owing to
the irregular, happy-go-lucky mode of life
that we have been compelled to lead during

the last five or six years, you have got out
of the tradition of your class. You have
assimilated a lot of cheap, modern, revolu-
tionary ideas. Armidis, with his preposterous
unconventionality, is to blame. I curse the
day when we first met him.'

Then he dwelt upon the manifold and
manifest virtues of the Prince; his wealth,
his rank, his celebrity, his good nature. But
finally and chiefly he appealed to my right
feeling, my sense of duty, as his daughter,
not to set myself up as the sole obstacle to
the consummation of his hopes in Russia.
And when I showed myself deaf and insensible even to this last appeal, he denounced
me as a monster of selfishness and ingratitude.

' Look at this miserable closet, this hole in
the wall, called a room, in which I, at my age,
with my tastes and habits, am constrained to
live and move and have my being! . . . I, who
was born in the lap of luxury; who from my

cradle until a few years ago was accustomed
to every phase of ease and pleasantness that
ingenuity could invent, and money purchase.
I, an old man, a failing man ! It is shortening my life, it is hurrying me to my grave !
I have endured it as long as I can. Every
day it becomes more and more humiliating,
more and more insupportable, to me. This
precarious, restricted, mean, ignoble manner
of existence ! A perpetual alternation between privation and hardship on the one
hand, and ignominy and mortification on the
other. And then to think that but for my
daughter, but for my own flesh and blood, I
might be relieved of all this to-morrow ! I
might to-morrow be reinstated in the enjoy-
ment of my own fortune and my own position
in my own country ! To think that it is due
to my own flesh and blood that I must pass
my declining years in poverty and exile ! It
is too much. In very deed, it is sharper

than a serpent's tooth to have a thankless child.'

'I suppose I *am* a monster of selfishness,' I began to think. 'Here, at any rate, it is certain that I have it in my power to procure my father all that he most desires. Yet I refuse to do so. Why? For no better reason, after all, than that it suits me better. In other words, I refuse to sacrifice my own will and pleasure for his. That is what is generally called selfishness. It is true that if I would marry Prince Léonticheff, my father's dearest dreams could be fulfilled.'

This thought began to prey upon me, to haunt me and torment me: that it was my fault, my fault alone, that my father had, as he said, to pass his declining years in poverty and exile. If I would, I could rescue him from them. I had but to speak one word, and honour and riches awaited him. Surely, I thought, it is selfish of me to refuse to

speak that word.   And yet I felt that I could
not speak it; that it was a difficulty of power,
more than one of will, that I could never
bring myself to speak it; that my lips would
refuse to shape it, my tongue to utter it.

'Remember, it is shortening my life. *You*
are shortening my life,' my father said.

'Oh, father, I can't do it, I can't do it,' I
groaned. 'I would do it, if I could; yes, if
I could, I believe I would; but I can't. It
is beyond my power. Don't look at me and
treat me and think of me as if I were
wantonly injuring you. I would do anything, anything, but that. But when I think
of Prince Léonticheff in that way, my whole
nature recoils; I loathe him and hate him,
and I hate myself. It is not my fault. I
can't do it, I can't. Oh, I wish you could
understand.'

'Oh, I understand, I quite understand; I
assure you it is not difficult to understand.

Go on. Continue. Sacrifice everything to your selfish weakness,' returned my father, contemptuously; and for three weeks after that he would not speak to me.

Then one day Prince Léonticheff announced to us that he was going to leave Paris. My heart leapt as if a great weight had been removed from it.

'I have an old engagement to take some English friends of mine off for a cruise on my yacht. We're bound for Norway, and we shall be gone all of August. I'll let you hear from me now and then. Early in September you may expect to see me again. Good-bye.'

'There,' said my father to me, after he had gone; 'you have done it at last. You have done what I feared. You have tired him out. There was a limit to his forbearance. Now he has gone. Farewell my hopes. Picture to yourself what I have to

thank you for. He will not come back.
You may congratulate yourself upon a pretty
stroke of business.'

I said nothing, but in my heart I thought,
'Alas, I am afraid he *will* come back.'

That was the first word my father had
spoken to me for three weeks. All through
the month of August he scarcely spoke to
me again.

Sometimes I would think, "After all, what
is the use? If it is a question of my happiness, am I not already as unhappy as unhappy
can be? The only thing I really care about,
I can never have. Already life is nothing to
me except a constant weary pain. Nothing
that could happen could make the pain any
greater. No, not even marriage with the
Prince. It would only be to change the
form of my misery; it would not add to it.
And—it would lift my father into the seventh

heaven of delight. As it is, I am of no use or value to any living human being, not even to myself. By consenting to marry the Prince, I should become of value to my father. Perhaps I had better do it.'

But then a vision of the Prince would shape itself before my imagination : his burly form, his hulking carriage, his fat, florid face, his complacent, ingratiating smile, his coarse red hands, all the hateful details of his person and his manner ; I would hear his monotonous, satisfied voice, husky and oily in the same breath ; and I would shrink from the thought of him with an overmastering, physical disgust, like a child whom people are urging to drink some nauseous medicine.

But even yet I did not believe him to be a vicious man. On the contrary, I still believed him to be at the core kind and well-meaning, though infinitely crude and unlovely on the surface, and unutterably tedious.

Though my father would not speak to me, he talked very freely to Armidis; and Armidis sometimes repeated what he said to me.

'He describes himself as quite frantic,' Armidis told me. 'Here,' he says, 'is a marriage offering itself, far more advantageous than any he could have hoped for you, even if you had retained your position in Russia; of course ten thousand times more brilliant still, in view of your actual circumstances; and you, in sheer whim and caprice, you set yourself against it. It is to fly in the face of Providence. It would try the patience of a saint. It is a piece of gross unreasoning selfishness, for which there is not even the shadow of an excuse. It is driving the poor man to despair. Oh, my ducats! Oh, my daughter! He thinks I am to blame. I have instilled ridiculous notions of independence into your little head.

Now he wishes me to speak with you, labour with you, use my influence with you, seek to bring you to reason, and to repair the mischief I have wrought : all which, you see, like the amiable and obliging fellow that I am, I do to the best of my poor ability.'

He said all this laughingly ; but now, 'Ah,' he cried, suddenly becoming grave, 'you are going through a few of the bitterest experiences a woman's life can hold. Forsaken,—or apparently forsaken,—by the man you love, and importuned to marry the man you don't love ! It is very hard, very hard, my dear. But keep up your courage, keep up your strength, and tire them out.'

'Yes,' I said, 'if they don't tire me out first.'

It was beginning to wear upon me, my father's policy of silent disapprobation. Treated all day long every day as if I had done something shameful and disgrace-

ful, never spoken to, and met constantly with
cold reproachful glances,—it was beginning
to be more than I could bear. It somehow
undermined my confidence in the righteous-
ness of my own cause, making me feel as if
I really had done something shameful and
disgraceful, so that I carried with me a heavy
sense of guilt, like an evil conscience.

‘Oh, I wish I were your father’s father,’
said Armidis.

‘Why do you wish that ?’ I questioned.

‘Oh, if I were his father, wouldn’t he
catch it, though! I’d give him something
that he’d remember all the rest of his life.
Haven’t you noticed the prodigal way in
which he has been adding to his wardrobe
lately ?’

No, I hadn’t noticed it. Was it so ?

‘You’re so self-absorbed you don’t notice
anything nowadays. Paul Mikhaelovitch has
been blossoming out in half a dozen new

suits of clothes. What I want to know is where he gets the funds.'

I went home, and I asked my father, 'Have you been borrowing money from Prince Léonticheff?'

'By what authority do you presume to question me?' returned my father.

'I want to know. I want you to tell me. Have you taken money from him?'

'I must decline to answer any such impertinent questions from my daughter,' he said.

But that was equivalent to an admission. My father had been borrowing money from the Prince! Did not this add a serious element of complication to the problems that I had to face?

'Will you tell me how much? Will you tell me how much you owe him?' I pleaded.

'I will not tell you anything. I will not talk with you. Until you come to me in a spirit of contrition, and beg my pardon for your selfish obstinacy, and offer me your obedience, you need not expect me to hold any intercourse with you.'

Towards the end of August I received the following letter from the Prince. It bore the Copenhagen post-mark. . . .

'DEAR MADEMOISELLE BANAKINE :—

'As you see by the date of this note, I am aboard the *Tchernobog*, off Copenhagen, on my way back to Paris from our cruise in these clear Scandinavian waters.

'You have no doubt observed that I am a very rough and awkward man with my tongue. Somehow it seems as though Nature had decreed that the pen should be my instinctive vehicle of expression. The moment I take my pen in hand, a change comes over my entire character. A load is lifted from

my mind, my faculties are unchained, my
vision becomes clearer, my thoughts become
keener, my feelings purer and better. And
I am like a dumb man suddenly blessed with
the gift of speech. I discover, to my surprise,
to my joy, that I can express myself faithfully; that I need no longer stumble and
stammer, and expose myself to miscon-
struction because of the imperfection and
ambiguity of my utterance, but that I can
say what I am moved to say in the way my
heart longs to say it.

‘Many times, many times, I have tried to
tell you that I love you; I have tried by
word of mouth to give vent to these deep
and strenuous emotions of passion and of
tenderness that have been stirring in my
heart of hearts ever since the day I first saw
you in Paris a few months ago. Will you
let me try once more to tell it to you, to tell
you that I love you and how I love you;

this time with my pen on paper? Love you! Love you! Oh, I love you so dearly, so dearly and tenderly, so entirely! There is nothing in my power, there is nothing that I can imagine, which I would not do to procure you a moment of happiness, or to save you from a moment of pain. I love you so dearly that at this moment I would cut off my own hand, if by doing so I could bring one ray of joy into your life, or expel from it a single pang of sorrow.

'I want you to become my wife. Oh, how my heart leaps as I write the words! My wife! You, Monica, my wife! I want you to become my wife. I want it first because I am human and therefore selfish; and I have come to love you so utterly that my only hope of happiness in this world depends upon you; so utterly that if you send me away from you, I shall feel like one going out into eternal darkness upon a measureless

desert of dry and arid sand : whereas if you
will take me to you, if you will accept me, all
my life will become one radiant glorious bless-
ing to me. But I want it secondly, because
there is an unselfish element in my love ; because I know I can make you happy. I can
make you happy and I can make your father
happy. And the whole world will be happier
and better for our great happiness.   Oh,
believe me, Monica ! Believe me and trust
me, and say that you will be my wife.

'I wish you to know this : that there is no
concession I will not make in order to win
you. Ask me anything, it shall be yours.
Impose any condition, I will submit to it.
No kinder husband ever existed than you
will find in me. I shall make it the sole aim
and occupation of my life to shelter and protect you, to serve you, to provide for you, to
cherish and keep you. And all I ask in
return is the privilege to call you by my

name, to look at you and think, She is my
wife, my wife!

'Do you believe I love you? Do you
believe in the seriousness and earnestness
and kindness of my love? How then can
you fear it or mistrust it? How can you
fear it or mistrust it? How can you hesitate
to give yourself to the keeping of a man who
loves you like that?

'Ah, but my love is unrequited! I tell
myself that a hundred times a day. She
does not love me, she does not love me! I
tell it to myself over and over; but it does
no good. My own love is so great and
ardent, I cannot be other than hopeful. For
see: you do not love me, but neither do you
hate me; and if you will only marry me, I
will be so good to you, so devoted, so faithful
and so tender, I will serve you so untiringly.
I will in one syllable make you so happy,
that in the end you cannot help but love me.

Oh, give me a chance to prove it to you.   If
you could look into my heart, and see with
your own eyes how true and pure, how
absolute and all-controlling, my love for you
is, you could not hold out against me, you
would not hesitate for an instant to confide
your happiness to me, you could not fear or
doubt such a love as that, you could not
withstand it or refuse it.

' I am coming to Paris to press my suit in
person.   I shall arrive during the first week
of September.   Do you wish to know the
question that is never absent from my mind ?
that repeats itself over and over in my
thoughts all day, that keeps me awake at
night, or if I sleep haunts my dreams ?   It
is this : Will she have me ?   Is there any
hope for me ?

' Until the first week in September !   Ah,
the time seems long.

' You are to give my best respects to your

father, and remember me kindly to Mr.
Armidis. And whatever happens, whatever
fate you reserve for me, believe me now and
always your devoted

'LÉONTICHEFF.'

A queer love-letter, surely ; perfervid ;
even comical ; but I could not smile at it.
All day long, after reading it, I went about
with a dull anguish in my heart, as if I had
been threatened with some hideous calamity,
and could not hope to escape it.

VIII.

ONE evening in the last week of August I came home from an errand across the river, and had rather a startling little experience.

It was intensely hot. I had walked all the way home, and had got very tired and very heated. I went up to my room. My room faced northward, so that it was protected from the sun; and the window had been open, and the blinds closed, all day; and it was deliciously fresh and cool.

I sat down to rest. I felt strangely tired, unduly tired; weak, languid, almost faint. I had a queer sensation of weight upon my chest, and of compression, as if it were bound in an excessively tight bandage. But I closed my eyes, and lay back in my chair ; and the air from the window swept over me, bringing a grateful, reviving coolness.

All at once I began to cough. It was a cough unlike any that I had ever had before, deeper, more violent. It seemed as if my lungs were full of glue. I could not breathe. I could do nothing but cough, cough, cough, to save myself from suffocation or strangulation. I remember I thought, ' Why, this is strange. I have not had a cold. What makes me cough like this ?'

Suddenly my coughing ceased. I reached for my handkerchief... What I saw in another minute upon my handkerchief turned me to ice from head to foot. It was blood, a great scarlet patch of blood, vivid as flame upon the white linen.

My heart stopped beating, and a horrible thrill of terror ran through all my body. It

was like suddenly hearing the voice of Death
in my ears, and feeling the glacial touch of
his hand.

I was utterly ignorant about such things.
Only in a general way I knew that hæmor-
rhage was considered a symptom of something alarmingly wrong in a person's health.
In my ignorance I thought, ' There ! I am
going to be ill, to have consumption, or
something... Oh, heavens, what shall we do
now ? What will become of us now ? If I
am going to fall ill, and be unable to work !'

What Prince Léonticheff had said came
back to my memory with awful force : ' Suppose your health should break down ? Eh ?'
His face rose before me, lit by a triumphant
smile, and seemed to question me : ' Well,
now ? What are you going to do ? Where
will your daily bread come from now ?'

The bleeding continued from time to time
throughout the night. I think I hardly need

to say that I suffered all the agonies that the imagination, stimulated by fear, and unrestrained by any sort of knowledge, can occasion one.

I did not wish to frighten my father, if it could be helped. So, in the morning, without telling him, I went to the consulting-room of Dr. Druot, who, I knew, was esteemed one of the ablest specialists in diseases of the lungs in Paris.

He put me through a long and fatiguing examination. In the end he said, ' I find a consolidation at the apex of the left lung. No, it is not a case for serious alarm, but it is a case for great care. If you are extremely careful, the consolidation may be resolved away. No, no, it is not consumption, not at all ; but if it were neglected, it would develop into consumption. You must leave Paris at once. You must go to the country : Switzerland I would recommend, or

the Tyrolean Alps. You must eat well,
sleep well, guard yourself religiously against
exposure to cold, and never allow yourself to
get in the slightest degree fatigued. It is
essential that your mind and body should
enjoy perfect repose. Any sort of strain,
bodily or mental, to which you might be
subjected, would tell instantly upon this weak
spot, this point of least resistance.'

'Yes, I understand,' I said. ' But suppose
I were too poor to do all this ? Suppose I
could not afford to leave Paris? That I
must stay here to do my daily work, and
earn my living ? What would become of me
then ?'

'Ah, madam, the people who get well of
troubles like this are those who are able to
take proper care of themselves. The others,
those who are in the predicament that you
describe, they are the ones who die.'

'Well, that is my predicament exactly,' I

said. 'I have no money except what I can
earn from day to day by teaching music.
Now I beg of you to be perfectly candid,
and tell me the worst.'

'If you wish me to be candid, I will say
that unless you take absolute rest, and great
care of yourself, you will probably become
an incurable consumptive within six months.'

'And if I do take that rest and that
care?'

'Oh, there is no reason why you should
not become perfectly well and strong, and
live to a green old age. You are not especially ill as yet; but according as you live a
life of ease or of hardship, you will get very
much better or very much worse within a
short period. If you continue to work, you
will have to go to the hospital before the
spring.'

So it reduced itself to this: I would no
longer be able to earn a livelihood for my

father and myself. In other words, destitution stared us in the face.

'The doctor forbids me to work. If I don't work, we starve. If I do work, I sicken, and perhaps die, and my father is left to starve alone,' I said to myself.

The corollaries were obvious.

I went home, and I said to my father, '*Soit!* I will marry Prince Léonticheff, if he will take me when he learns the condition of my health.'

*   *   *   *   *

'And now,' concluded Armidis,—he had come to me in a great state of indignation and excitement, to ask, 'Is this true, that your father tells me?' and when I had answered, 'Yes, it is quite true,' he had talked with me, reasoned with me, pleaded with me, for an hour, trying, as he said, to save me from myself; but my mind was made up, and I had listened to him with

incredulity and obstinacy, fool, fool, fool that
I was,—'And now,' he concluded, 'it will be
your own doing, your own fault. You will
have no one but yourself to blame for all the
unutterable misery that you are going to
bring upon yourself. I tell you that a loveless marriage is the worst sin, the worst
sacrilege, that a human being can be guilty
of. Nothing can justify it, nothing. It is a
violation, a degradation, a profanation of
everything that is fine or good or sweet, of
everything that is sacred, in human nature.
How you can bear the thought of it I cannot
understand. I should think you would
rather die a thousand times. Look : I will
use plain words with you. You are no
longer a child, and I can use plain words
with you. Well, then, I say it is worse, it is
immeasurably worse, than prostitution : for
prostitution is but for the hour or for the
day, whereas this frightful marriage is for

life. Oh, my God! Monica, Monica! Oh,
where is your soul? Where are your
instincts, your intuitions?'

He walked rapidly up and down the room,
wringing his hands, breathing heavily. I
sat still in my chair, looking hard at the floor,
determined to let nothing that he could say
alter my resolution.

'Listen to me,' he went on. 'There never
yet was a loveless marriage made that didn't
end in wretchedness, not only for the woman,
but for every one in any way concerned. It
isn't only your own happiness, and Julian
North's happiness, that you're dealing a
death-blow to, it is just as surely your
father's happiness, Léonticheff's happiness,
the happiness of your unborn children. Your
children who will come into this world conceived not in love, but in a man's lust, and
a woman's loathing! And Léonticheff's happiness, I say. No, even if, instead of being

the brute beast that he is, even if he were
the purest and the most honourable gentleman in the world, not loving him, you would
have no right to marry him ; not loving him,
if you married him, you would do him, him
as well as yourself, a great wrong ; you would
engulph him and yourself, and your unborn
children, and everybody else concerned, in
hopeless misery.   Not loving him, you have
no right to marry him.   How much less
right have you to marry him, when you do
love another man !   Oh, I tremble for you,
I tremble for you.   But I have done my
utmost to save you, and now it will be your
own fault. . .   Oh, I know, I know what you
are going to say,' he cried, as I started to
interrupt him.   'I know, I know !   Julian
North does not love you any more !   He
has neglected you, he has abandoned you !
I don't believe it, I have told you a hundred
times that I don't believe it ; but I will grant

it for the sake of the argument; and then,
What of it? What of it? Do two wrongs
make a right? So long as one last particle
of tenderness for him, of regret for him,
lingers in your heart, you have no right even
to dream of marrying another man. Oh, is
there nothing that I can say, nothing that
I can do, to move you, to bring you to
reason, to wake you up, and rescue you from
this utter ruin? Oh, it is like a nightmare.
I see you in extreme peril, but unconscious
of your peril, and I long with all my strength
to warn you, to save you; but when I call
out to you, you refuse to hear me, you are
deaf and insensible. It is a question of
ways and means? It is to avoid destitution? You cannot work any more, and if
you don't work, starvation stares you in
the face, you and your father? Don't I tell
you that I will never let you want, you or
your father? Don't I tell you that so long

as I have a shilling in my pocket, half of it
will be for you ?   Oh, you can't accept help
from me ! You would rather sell yourself
body and soul to the devil, than accept help
from me, from a friend who loves you like
his own child, from one who has five times
more money than he needs to spend, and
would never feel the difference !   You would
rather sell your soul to the devil, and make
your body over as a chattel to Léonticheff !
Oh, you drive me mad, you drive me frantic.
I see you in this great peril, and I see that
you do not realise your peril, and I signal
to you and call out to you, and you are deaf
and blind, and I know that in a little while
you will have wrecked your life, wrecked it
for ever.   I believe,—I do honestly believe,
—it would be better if I should kill you.
Better if I should kill you here, now, on the
spot !'

'I wish you would, I wish you would,' I

cried. 'But if you don't kill me, if no one
kills me, if I have to live, then...'

'Then it will be your own fault, I say. If
you marry Prince Léonticheff, it will be of
your own free will, with your eyes open, and
the consequences will be your own fault. I
have shown you all the true morality of the
matter as clearly as speech can do it. I
have offered you every means of escape.
Now, if you do it, you do it of your own
free will, in perfect knowledge and understanding of what you are doing, and of what
must inevitably follow. You are deliberately
choosing to sow the wind, and you are perfectly aware that you must reap the whirl-
wind. Now I will say no more. I have
done. I have tried to save you from destroying your happiness, but that is not all.
I have tried to save you also from destroying
your soul, from debasing and polluting your
soul. Happiness doesn't matter so very

much, perhaps; perhaps you could never have been entirely happy; but your soul...! The soul that God has entrusted to your keeping! What right have you to ruin that? Oh, I tell you, the worst part of such pain as you are storing up for yourself is not that it is hot and biting and hard to bear: the worst part of it is that it demoralises the soul, that it corrupts and diseases and dis-integrates the soul. Yes, pain of that sort is infinitely, irresistibly demoralising. Mark what I say, and learn in good time how true it is. Watch the gradual demoralisation that will come upon you, creep upon you, grow upon you, from the day of your wedding to the end. Oh, I know the process: it is thus. I want to be happy; I have keen and strong in me the craving for happiness that is common and intrinsic to human nature, like the craving for food, for drink, for air. But I have done that which puts happiness for-

ever beyond my reach. I have sold my
birthright in happiness for a mess of pottage.
I have made a bargain whereby I have
renounced all claim to happiness, though I
have obtained nothing in compensation.
Very good, very good; now look. All this
time the craving for happiness is there in
·my heart, gnawing like hunger, burning like
thirst. It begins to be unendurable. This
bargain that I have made I have got the
worst of; this renunciation, I begin to think,
is artificial, is unnatural, is unjust; this de-
privation is unreasonable, uncompensated,
impossible. I brood upon it, brood upon
it; and by and by my brooding reaches the
ear of the devil, like a voice summoning
him, and he comes to me. He says to me,
"How is this? You crave happiness, but
you have sold your claim to it. So! By
fair means, then, it appears, you can't hope
to obtain it. Well, then, why not try foul

means? Why not try to steal a little of it back?" And the instant the Tempter first puts that question to me, that instant I begin to go to pieces, my moral disintegration sets in. His breath upon my conscience has pro-duced a little spot of corruption, of gangrene; and now it begins to spread. I cannot obtain happiness by fair means; well, then, why be too scrupulous about the means?... You doubt what I say? It is a fancy, a phrase? Very good. Have it so if you like. Ten years hence, five years hence, I will ask you for your maturer opinion. Meantime, oh, God pity you!'

*　　*　　*　　*　　*

The Prince went with us as far as Geneva. There he left us, for what he called a little run into Russia. At the end of six weeks he came back, bearing two important docu-ments. One was a full and free pardon for my father, restoring him to all his rights as

a Russian nobleman, including the possession of his sequestrated estates; the other
was an Imperial authorisation of our marriage.

We were married at Nice, in December.
Then my father bade us good-bye, and returned to St.-Petersburg.

PART IV.

MATRIMONY.

I.

EARLY in May, 1890, we came on to London, to pass the Season at Salchester House. A few days after our arrival, however, Prince Léonticheff went away again. He said to me, ' I shall probably be gone a fortnight or three weeks.' But he did not tell me where he was going.

We had been married more than four years. It is essential to the purposes of this confession that I should now set down as accurately and as dispassionately as possible the conception of Prince Léonticheff's character which I had come to entertain as a result of those four years of close acquaintance with him ; also that I should summarise briefly the history of our married life ; and finally that I should explain the actual state of our relations to each other.

My greatest difficulty will be to do justice to Prince Léonticheff.

I feel that unless this story that I am trying to tell, be, in all its aspects, in all its details, in all its inferences and implications, as true as human endeavour can make it, then it will destroy its own *raison d'être*, it will defeat itself ; and all the time and labour that I have given it will have been expended in vain. And especially, if I err in my account of Prince Léonticheff, if the picture I present of him be false in colour or distorted in form, I might as well, I might better, have held my peace.

I should find it easy enough to say in three words : I was miserably, incredibly unhappy ; he treated me with the grossest brutality, the most refined cruelty; I hated him, I loathed him; he was bad, bad, bad. And all this would be true, in a way; but it would be only a fraction of the truth; it would be the truth seen from only one angle; and in its effect it would equal a falsehood.

For my own sake, if for no better reason, I must try to suppress my personal feelings, and to make my testimony concerning him impartial and discriminating.

To begin with, then, I must admit that he was not entirely bad, not by any means entirely bad. To this it might be answered that no human being ever was entirely bad, or entirely good; that absolute perfection or absolute depravity are no more attainable in flesh and blood, than a mathematically perfect line or circle is attainable with ink and paper; that in the heart of the most spotless saint or the most exalted hero there must lurk some remaining traces of human wickedness or weakness, whilst in that of the most vicious evil-doer some remote, perhaps microscopic, fibre must survive not wholly corrupt.... But when I say of Prince Léonticheff that he was not entirely bad, I do not mean it in that niggard philosophic sense. I mean that in an appreciable number of his actions and impulses he was positively good. Indeed, if I could leave his relations with me out of the question, I should be obliged to declare that, on the whole, as men go, he was not much worse than the average. So long as he was comfortable in mind and body, so long as he had his own way, and his appetites were satisfied, he really was a good-natured and well-meaning person. With money, for example, he was extremely free-handed, giving large sums annually to many charities, lending large sums to relieve the embarrassments

of his friends, and always readily drawing
his purse from his pocket when any case
of distress among the poor was brought to
his notice. If physical courage be a virtue,
he had it in abundance. To give but a
single instance, when malignant typhus was
raging in south-eastern Russia, in the summer
of 1886, he left London at the height of the
Season, and went straight to the district
where the pestilence was doing its worst,
and remained there for more than a month,
visiting the hospitals, distributing alms, and
writing descriptions of the horrors that he
witnessed, for the English public to read in
his newspaper, the *Beacon*. ... He was
coarse, if you please, and vulgar, and fatuous
to the verge of insanity ; he was clumsy and
heavy and tactless ; he was so completely
wrapped up in himself that he never thought
to avoid offending the sentiments of his
neighbours : but his usual condition of mind

was, none the less, one of lazy smiling con-
tentment, the outward and visible sign of
which was a broad and imperturbable good-
nature.

Yes, if his relations with me could be
eliminated from the problem, I believe I
should have to say of him that, despite his
conceit and his vulgarity, taken for all in all,
and tried by the ordinary standards of the
world, he was not much worse than the
average of men.

A point upon which I must bear is this :
that he thoroughly and profoundly believed
himself to be, not merely no worse than the
average man, but far, far better. He
thoroughly believed himself to be a paragon
of all manly virtue. He was no cynic, no
hypocrite. He admired the nobility of his
own character as fervently and as sincerely
as he admired the power and acumen of his
own intellect,—with a sincerity and a fervour

indeed, that were almost religious. I am sure that under no possible circumstances would he ever have done anything that he thought brutal, or mean, or wrong. But then, he always thought, earnestly and honestly thought, that what he desired to do was right. That,—or, in other words, his total lack of humour,—was the key to his personality. Lacking humour, he lacked all sense of perspective, of congruity, of proportion, in looking at life. He regarded himself as the Centre of the Universe, the Fact of supreme significance in the world; his wish, his idea, his sensation of the moment was the one thing of real importance. If you opposed his wish, or disputed his idea, or caused him a disagreeable sensation, he believed in all conscience that you were a double-dyed villain, actuated by the basest motives, and attempting a most horrid crime; and that he was not simply justified, but that he was morally bound, to go to any length, to employ any means, for the purpose of vanquishing you, of confuting and confounding you, and defeating your nefarious designs.

I said long ago that the results of his lack of humour upon his conduct, often queer, were sometimes appalling. I believe that his lack of humour was accountable for the very worst meannesses, brutalities, and cruelties of which he was ever guilty, as well as for his most ridiculous solecisms. When, for instance, he would strike his wife, I am convinced that he believed himself to be performing an unpleasant but righteous duty, just as a father at times believes it to be his duty to administer corporal punishment to a refractory child.

At the time of our betrothal I had said very explicitly to the Prince—what, for the rest, it was scarcely necessary to say—' It must be understood that I do not love you, that I can never love you.'

'Oh, that will be all right,' said he. 'You don't love me now, and I don't ask you to. But you will love me, you will come to love me. You can't help loving me, when once I've had a chance to woo you. I'm not at all disturbed about that.'

'I assure you, you are deceiving yourself,' I responded. 'If you choose to marry a woman who does not love you, well and good. It is your own affair. But you mustn't delude yourself with the fancy that I shall come to love you. I never shall, I never can. It is best that you should make up your mind to that now, at the outset. Otherwise, you will prepare a disappointment for yourself.'

But he had chosen not to heed this warning, not to give it any weight or place in his calculations. He believed that his powers

of fascination were altogether irresistible,
and that no woman could help succumbing
to them, if they were once brought to bear
upon her, any more than she could help
drowning if she were immersed in water.
Herein lay the beginning of much of our
trouble.   For awhile after our marriage, I
must do him the justice of saying, no man
could have been more patient or more forbearing with a woman's indifference than he
was with mine. . . .

'Now that I have won your hand, you
must let me win your heart,' he said. 'When
you have seen how truly and devotedly I
love you, how eager I am to make you
happy, how untiring I will be in your service,
how kind I shall be, how I shall have no
other purpose in life than that of contri-
buting in some way to your happiness and
your well-being, I am sure your heart cannot
hold out against me.'

And for the first winter after our marriage, I must confess, there was nothing in his conduct, nothing even in his speech, of which I could fairly complain ; on the contrary, nothing but what, remembering always that I was his wife, and he my husband, nothing but what deserved, even if it didn't obtain, my gratitude and my praise. He was on his good behaviour. In his speech he subdued and mitigated himself to such a degree that one who had not known him before would perhaps never have thought of him as an especially unrefined or under-bred man. And in his conduct he was certainly all that I had any right to expect, considering our relations—considering that I had sold myself to him, and was his wife. He was indeed untiring in his efforts to serve me, to make me happy ; and if I remained miserably unhappy, if I was unhappier than I had ever been before, than I had ever

conceived of being, it was not his fault; it
was the fault of the situation, and the situation was the result of a bargain that I
myself had made. He had the tact and
the delicacy—incongruous as it may seem
to speak of tact and delicacy in connection
with Prince Léonticheff—he had the tact
and the delicacy seldom to obtrude himself
upon me. If he saw that his attentions were
unwelcome to me, he would suspend them;
that his talk was unwelcome, he would be
silent; that his presence was unwelcome,
he would go away and leave me alone. I
say, 'If he saw,' for unless a thing of that
sort were extremely plain, he could not see
it; and I generally would try not to let
him see.

'I never believed that he was a villain, but
now I know that he is really, according to
his light, a good man; far kinder and better
than I ever gave him credit for.' I began

to say to myself; and if I still could not
like him, if I felt no gratitude towards him,
I began at least to respect him and admire
him.

We spent that winter in his villa at Nice,
my health making it impossible for us to
go to Russia. We would never meet till
the afternoon. His mornings he passed in
his study, writing. After the mid-day breakfast he would usually come to see me in my
apartments, often bringing his manuscripts
with him to read them to me. Then he
would ask, 'And how would you like to
spend the afternoon?' Whatsoever wish I
expressed in answer to this question, he
bowed to without a murmur. If I mastered
my repugnance for his company enough to
say, 'I will go for a drive with you,' or
what else of the sort, it was almost touching
to witness his suppressed delight. If I said,
'I should like to be alone this afternoon,'

he would answer, 'Very well,' and submissively withdraw. He was surely as kind, as forbearing, as I, whom he had regularly bought and paid for, who bore his name, and ate his bread, and was his wife, had any right to expect.

'No,' I said to myself, 'it is not Prince Léonticheff whom I must blame, it is the situation, and the situation is one of my own making. If I had to sell myself at all, I could scarcely have sold myself to a better man than Prince Léonticheff.' And my wonder was great that so clear-sighted a person as Armidis could have formed so mistaken an estimate of him.

But all the same, the situation was an extremely painful one, a most terrible and hateful one, and I was very far from happy in it. I would look at those other women, of the half-world, who throng the Riviera at this season, and I would realise that after all the difference between them and me was not a moral difference, was only a conventional difference; and my heart would burn, and I could not lift up my eyes. Would I some time become accustomed to it, and not mind it any more, like them ? I understood with a sort of sick horror that that sort of relief would be worse than the pain itself; that it would mean the final death and corruption of whatever remained pure and clean in my soul.

Oh, I was very far from happy. I had determined to put the thought of Julian North absolutely out of my mind, the love of him absolutely out of my heart. Perhaps I had succeeded in doing so ; but it had been a little like tearing out a living fibre, and it left a wound that ached. It had been, too, like taking away from my life the only thing that made life worth living, the only thing that gave me an object to hope for, to work and wait for, to look forward to : now my life was all meaningless, purposeless, insipid to me; and as I realised how irrevocable it was, and how it must go on like this, without aim, without savour, for who could tell how many years—probably until I died, an old, old woman,—I could not help it, but I fell to asking, 'What is the use? Wherein is it worth while? Oh, have I got to plod this dismal circle round and round until I die?' Sometimes these questions would simply depress me, and fill me with a sort of dull languid despair; but at other times they would infuriate me, madden me, with hurt and resentment. 'Here is my one life,' I would cry, 'my one precious life, mine for once in the course of all time; and must I sit still, with hands tied, like Tantalus, and see it slip by, just beyond my reach, unemployed and unenjoyed? Of no use, interest, or profit to a single living human being, least of all myself! Is this what I was born for? Is it for this that life was given me? Life, precious, mysterious life! Must it be squandered in pettinesses, in fruitless and flavourless nothings, when it is not scorched and withered with pain and shame? Oh, I would rather die at once.'

At first I had tried to find some solace, some oblivion, some excitement, in the doings of society, and in the chances of Monte Carlo. At first I had not altogether failed ; but as soon as the novelty wore off, gambling began to pall, and society to wear, upon me. I was not very strong, and dressing and going, going and dressing, fatigued me ; and besides, the Russian and English people who made up our world, were one and all either the fastest of the fast, or the slowest of the slow : in both cases equally unsatisfactory.

But as the spring drew near, Prince

Léonticheff's patience began to show signs of giving way. He had tried all winter long to move my heart, and win my love. So long as he had been able to hope that by kindness he might prevail, he had been kind. If I could have loved him, I do not doubt, he would have continued kind. But I could not love him; and now, as he began to lose hope, as he began to think that perhaps I might never love him, his attitude towards me, and his treatment of me, began to alter.

At the outset, however, the alteration was not greatly for the worse. His attitude acquired a certain expression of injury, of righteous long-suffering, as if I had wantonly sinned against him, and he was sorry, rather than angry. His treatment of me became a little less *empressé*, and seemed to imply a reproach, as if I were a perverse child, and my perversity grieved him. The germ of all our trouble lay in this : Prince Léonticheff

was utterly unable to understand that I *could*
not love him ; that it was with me not a
question of willingness, but a question of
power ; that I had no more power to change
the nature of my feeling towards him, than I
had to change the colour of my eyes. He
was utterly unable to understand that. As
undoubtingly as he believed that he lived
and breathed, so undoubtingly also did he
believe that no woman upon whom he chose
to exert his charms could help loving him,
if she would only let herself go ; and his
inference was that I, perversely, deliberately,
of malice aforethought, was holding myself
back, was checking the natural tendency of
my emotions, and laboriously compelling
myself to remain indifferent to him. Believing this, he not unnaturally felt aggrieved,
felt that I was cheating him of what he had
earned, that I was withholding from him his
due, that I was of set purpose refusing him

justice ; and he commenced to regard himself as a wronged man, a sort of martyr, and me as a cold-hearted, wicked woman.

His attitude towards me, and his treatment of me, as I say, implied a grievance and a reproach ; but it was a long while before he spoke.   We left Nice in May, 1886, to come to London.   It was in the train, in the seclusion of a Pullman compartment, as we were nearing Calais, that he first broached the subject of his wrongs.

'Look here, Monica,' he said, 'I want to have a little talk with you.   I want to have a little serious talk with you, if you don't mind. I think you will be fair enough to acknowledge that I haven't ⸰troubled you much this winter with talk about ourselves, and now perhaps you can endure a little. There are things that ought to be said.'

'Yes ?' I answered, in a flutter of nervous apprehension.

'Well, to begin with, I know it would be utterly useless for me to ask you whether you care anything for me. I know you don't. You don't care a halfpenny for me, you don't care a farthing. I'm as fond of you, as careful of you, as kind to you, as a man can be to a woman, and yet you don't care any more for me, you haven't any more ordinary affection for me, not to speak of love, than you have for the engine-driver of this train.'

He paused for a little; but I kept my eyes turned from him, and did not speak; and by and by he resumed...

'All this winter long I have done everything in my power, everything I could think of, to make you happy, to make you comfortable and contented, and to move your heart a little towards me. Whatever wish you have expressed, or I have been able to divine, has been law to me. I've never

asked a single service of any kind from you ;
and when you have chosen to do me one
unasked, I have accepted it with thankful-
ness, as if, instead of being my due, it were
a gratuitous favour on your part. I have
always preferred your pleasure not only to
my pleasure, but to my interests. I know,
for instance, that some of my best friends,
some of my most valuable and useful friends,
have been offended this winter by our
neglect of them. But I saw that you didn't
care for them, that it would be a bore for
you to have to visit them much, or entertain
them; and so I said nothing, I made no
protest or complaint, I let you go your own
way, and ignore them. I only mention that
as an example of what I mean when I say
that I've made no demands upon you, that
in small things as well as great I've respected
your pleasure as if it were the only thing of
importance in the world.'

'Yes,' I said. 'You have been very good, very patient and forbearing. But I did not mean to offend your friends. If I had known that you cared about it, I should have been perfectly willing to receive them and visit them as often as you liked. I simply waited for you to express your desire.'

'Quite so, quite so. Don't understand me as complaining of your conduct. I'm not complaining of it, I'm only reminding you of it. You waited for me to express my desire ; but I *didn't* express my desire, I *suppressed* it, because I wanted to spare you even the faintest sort of fatigue or annoyance. The thing I do complain of is this. First, that you appear deliberately to have shut your heart against me, to have hardened yourself against me, so that you haven't given me,—all I ask for,—a fair chance to win you, or yourself a fair chance to be won.

You seem to have made up your mind
beforehand that you will deliberately prevent
any particle of liking or fondness for me,
not to speak of passionate love, taking root
in your heart. All I've done, and all I've
refrained from doing, don't appear to have
made any impression of any kind upon you.
You have simply set to work with might
and main to freeze yourself towards me.
I must say I think I'm justified in complaining of that.'

'If it were true, yes, you would be justified
in complaining. But it is not true. I told
you before we were married that I did not
love you, that I never could love you. You
ought not to have married me, if you could
not be satisfied with that. I appreciate
deeply all your kindness to me this winter,
all your forbearance. But I can't love you.
It is no more possible for me to force a

feeling in my heart, than to force myself to grow an inch in stature.'

The blood rushed to his face, and he cried out, ' That's what makes me furious. I say that is downright childish folly. Nobody asks you to force a feeling in your heart. On the contrary, all I ask is that you will let your heart alone, let it follow its natural impulses. It isn't in nature for a woman to remain indifferent to a man who loves her as I love you, who is as kind to her, as untiring in his devotion to her, as I am to you. The trouble is that you're forcing your heart in the other direction. Let your heart alone, give your heart a chance. That's all I ask. Why, you couldn't help loving me, if you only wouldn't try not to. It makes me furious. Isn't it your duty to love your husband ? Isn't it his right to demand your love ? You say you can't force yourself to love him. Well, I tell you that if the man

is the sort of man I am, kind, and devoted,
and—I use your own words—forbearing and
patient, if he lays his life and his heart at
your feet as I do, I tell you you can't help
loving him, unless you make a deliberate
effort not to. And that's what you're doing,
and that's one of the things that I complain of.'

He was very much excited. He spoke in
a very loud voice, and very vehemently.
What could I answer? I looked out of the
window, and held my tongue.

'Well? well? Have you nothing to say?'
he demanded.

'I can't say any more than I have said. I
am not forcing my heart in any way. I can't
love you. I may esteem you and respect
you, but I can't love you. I told you I
couldn't at the outset. I told you you were
storing up a disappointment for yourself.
Why did you marry me?'

Again the blood rushed to his face, staining it almost purple. He bit his lips, his eyes flashed, and he cried out, ' By God ! Don't you ask me that again, or I'll do something we'll both be sorry for. I talk to you as if you were a sensible woman, and reason with you till I'm black in the face, and then I ask you what you have to answer, and you simply go back, like a little deaf, dumb, imbecile infant, and repeat what you said in the beginning, letter for letter, for all the world as if you hadn't heard a word that I had spoken. You —you ought to be taken out and whipped.'

' Why don't you take me out and whip me ?' I asked. I also was somewhat angry now.

' You'd better not tempt me to. Perhaps I will,' he retorted, nodding his head threateningly, and looking wickedly at me from his deep-set little eyes.

After which we were both silent for a while.

By and by he began again, very quietly . . .

' Of course I ought not to have said that, and I offer you my apologies. I'm sincerely sorry for it; but you infuriated me, and I didn't realise what I was doing. I'll say no more now about your loving me. I'll simply wait, and try, and hope. If you'll only give yourself and me a chance, I am sure you must come to love me in the end. But now there's something else I want to talk to you about; and that's the way you mope. Here you have everything in this world that a reasonable human being can ask for of the gods. You've got wealth, and all that wealth can buy; you've got a magnificent title, and a high place in the best society of Europe; you're not very strong, perhaps, but you've got no real disease, and on the whole you're blessed with health as good as that of most people; your time is all your own, to do with as you please; you've got a husband

who loves you like a dog, and whose only
purpose in life is to make you happy ; if any
woman ever had reason to be contented with
her lot, to thank heaven for her lot, you have.
And yet, see. Day after day you go about
with a rueful countenance, and a whining
voice, and pathetic eyes, to all appearances
miserably and morbidly wretched. Now I
complain that that is unreasonable, and
ungrateful, and unworthy of you. You have
no right to nurse misery, and refuse comfort.
It's your duty to enjoy and be thankful for
the good things that heaven has vouchsafed
you. And I say that if you go on like this,
you'll deserve to have some real misfortune
happen to you, just to punish you for your
ingratitude.'

I did not answer.

'Well, will you do me the honour of
answering me ?' he demanded.

'I have nothing to answer. I was not

aware that I had troubled you with any expression of my griefs, if I have griefs.'

'No, you haven't; and that's just the point. You go about with a dismal countenance, but you never speak. Now I say that if you have no griefs, then you'd better try to be and to look a little more cheerful. And if you have griefs, then I think it's my right to know what they are. I say you have no occasion for any griefs; but apparently you're eaten up by them, all the same; and now I demand to hear what they are. Good heavens, how many women in this world would like to change places with you!'

'If I have griefs, they are not ones that I can talk about. I did not know that my countenance had been dismal. I'll try to alter it.'

'It isn't your countenance that I complain of, except as your countenance reflects your heart. I say you have every possible reason to be light-hearted and happy. And if you're not that, if there is any deep and mysterious sorrow gnawing at your vitals '—this in a tone of irony—' I have a right to know what it is.'

' I do not think there is any deep or mysterious sorrow gnawing at my vitals. But if I am not exuberantly happy, I can't help it. One can't be happy or unhappy at will, any more than one can be hungry or thirsty. At least I can't.'

. ' Well, you wait. Perhaps some day you'll really have something to cry about. Then you will look back at this time, and wish with all your might that you'd realised how well off you were. Yes, by Jove, you're exactly like a child. You don't appear to have any more mind or reasoning faculty than a six-year-old infant. I might as well argue with an infant. Yes, by God! I was right. A

28—2

whipping would do you good. It would be
the only way of appealing to you, just as it's
the only way of appealing to a child. It
would set your blood circulating, and it would
take your mind off your imaginary, manu-
factured sorrows, to make acquaintance with
a little genuine pain.'.

'Thank you,' I returned.

'Well, now, then, I ask you once for all,
will you tell me what it is? If you've got
any grief of any kind in your bosom, I
demand to be told what it is.'

'I have nothing to tell you.'

'God damn you!' he screamed, his rage
suddenly getting the mastery of him. 'I
believe you are still thinking of that starved
cur of an American painter. If you are, by
God, I advise you to put the thought out of
your head, or there'll be trouble.'

I sprang to my feet, and made for the
door of the little Pullman compartment in

which we were travelling. But he placed himself before me.

'No, you may just sit down again where you were,' he said. 'If I want to talk to you, I think you may do me the honour to listen to me. There's no use your standing there. You don't leave this compartment till I'm ready to let you.'

'Oh, very well. If you resort to force. Of course you are stronger than I am,' I answered, and resumed my seat.

'Well, now, if you're ready, we may talk,' said he. 'And I want you to understand to begin with that I meant no offence to you by what I said about your young American painter. I spoke hotly, because you angered me; but you have no ground for taking offence. I will say this much for you at once: I know you are the soul of honour, and that you would never do anything to injure me. So far as that's concerned, I'd be perfectly willing to leave you alone with him on a desert island; I know you'd never be guilty of doing anything wrong; you've got too much honour, and too much pride and self-respect. But what I want to impress upon you is this: that you can injure me just as much by feeling and thinking, as you can by doing. I'm your husband, and your husband is entitled to demand of you not only that you should keep yourself faithful to him with your body, but also that you should be faithful to him in thought and feeling. Now, I submit it to you in all fairness, if it's your American painter who's standing between you and me, who's preventing you from giving me your love, isn't it due to me that you should put the thought of him entirely out of your mind? There, I have spoken to you reasonably and kindly; I expect a reasonable answer.'

'I will not answer you. I will not have

anything to say to you. You have insulted me and outraged me in the most cowardly manner; and you have compelled me by force, against my will, to sit here and listen to you. But you cannot compel me to answer you. I have nothing to say to you, except this : that, after the way in which you have spoken to me and treated me to-day, I despise you.'

'You hell-cat!' he cried, and struck me across the face.

END OF VOL. II.

BILLING AND SONS, PRINTERS, GUILDFORD.